The Walking Man

THE WOODS

MARK RELIC

SWEETSPIRE LITERATURE
MANAGEMENT

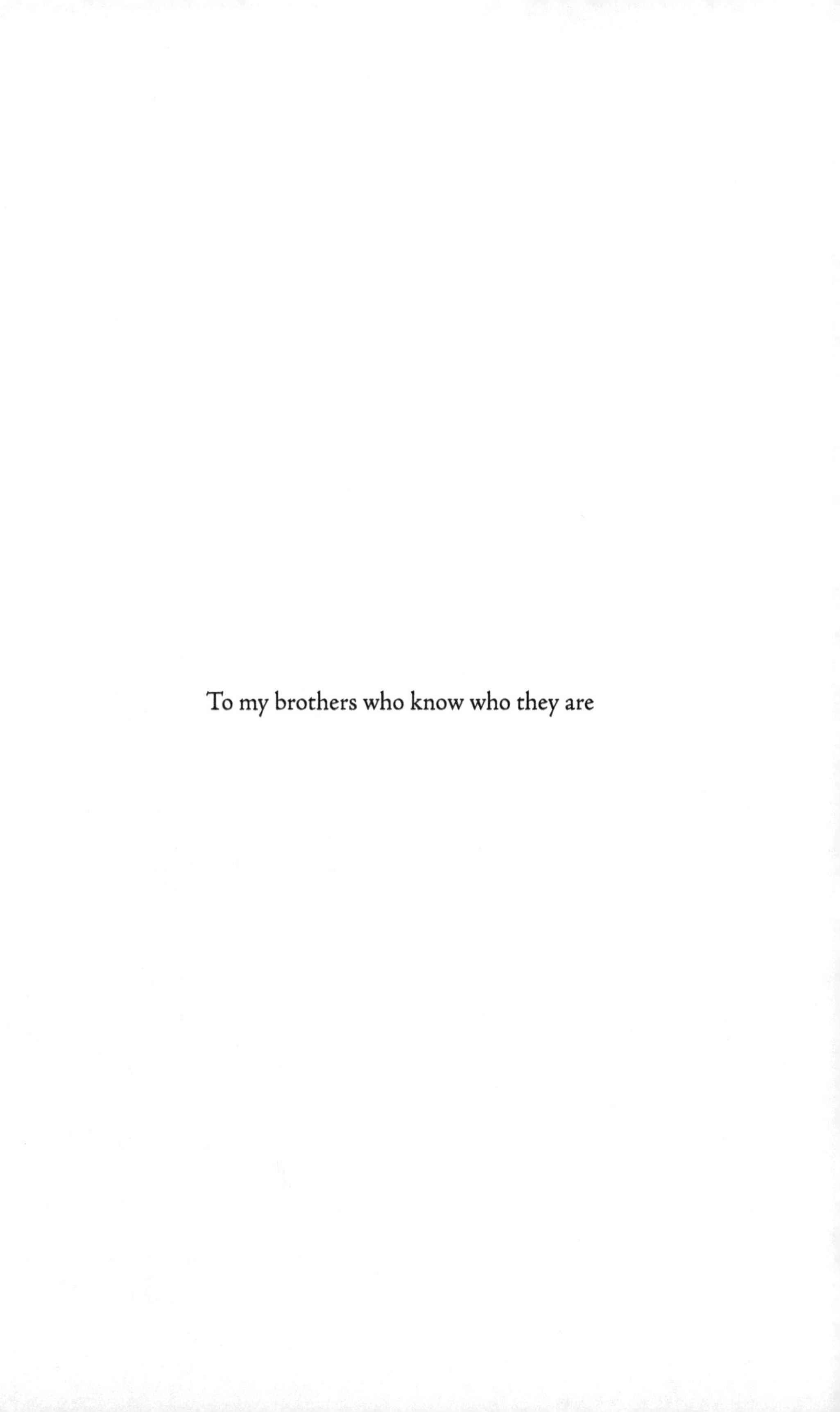

To my brothers who know who they are

I never trusted so called "reality" so I came up with my own.

The following is based on a true story.

Being lost is a part of life. It's a part of being human.
How far can you get lost, and find yourself again?
How many times can you fall to rise again, and again?

Life is hard, you say…
Well, you are right.
Every single thing comes from the mind…
That is amazing. Mind is amazing. Like the universe.
I'm not a preacher, nothing like that…
I'm sort of free-will if I use the words to describe me.
You can believe in me or not. That's totally up to you.
I am here to help you and will try to do so.
So just relax and clear your mind.
Arm yourself with patience. You'll need it.
Let's start with a smile.

Chapter 1

It's raining outside. It rains for days. The sky is a wide, dark-gray horizon. I listen to rain falling on gutters, trees, and leaves. I look through the window. It's quiet. I look at the glassy ball, a souvenir of Venice I got from a friend of mine for my birthday. I flip it upside down in my hand, looking at the white flakes that shatter.

For a while I thought about how I would start and kind of went along with how it actually happened. There is no simple way. There is no other time but present. There is no what has happened. Nor what will happen. There is only what's happening right now.

Part of the reason why I'm doing this is because I don't really know what is going to happen to me. What and how is going to be. The only thing I know is what's happening now. Although I'm not sure in anything except, I guess, in what I'm doing with these words... which I don't really know where will take me.

Written words are the identity of what I am while I'm writing. Kind of like a certain power of an odd feeling of truth that takes me over. Every word is some sort of a new start. Every thought is life for itself. It's not easy with words. It doesn't get easy, just different. It's a struggle although it may seem like not that big of a deal. I can't quite explain it. It comes like some sense of realization, a feeling of recognition. Puzzle.

What is the truth? What is reality? The one for which we all think we know what it is.

I've heard from someone recently that nobody cares for reality any more.

So who are we? What do our lives mean? What is our true purpose? What do we mean? We get born, we die and no one knows why.

Anyone? Anyone out there? Anyone at all…

Life, allegedly, simply came to be. And now we have a confusion of all that's happening today in the world of now. How to talk about it?

Modern technology is advancing very fast. It is taking its toll. It changed everything. It changed the world. It changed consciousness. And now everybody has their way of being or becoming somebody. I guess it's more fun to be somebody than to be nobody. All that by its nature becomes or ends up being disturbing. Scary even but no one seems to care. Everything is taken for granted like nothing matters. World became a cruel, terrifying and dangerous place.

Someone once said we are not complete human beings until we overcome all aspects of our lives. That's how that sounded. That same someone wrote that in his book about a man who gets bored by his life routine deciding that his life and decisions gets direction by flipping a dice. That dice like that book changed his life.

It is all about dancing, making a step after every next one. People think they know how to do it. They behave inferior to each other. People are divided. They are characterized by big differences. In a certain way they can be compared with animals.

It is all in perception, they say, the state of mind of how we see things. The way we realize them, except them. Excepting is a certain relief. I wonder how many people feel "relieved" right now.

It is all, allegedly, connected somehow. Earth is spinning. The world evolves.

Certain things happen in a certain time. People meet each other, they connect. They do all kinds of stuff together. That is, by its nature, beautiful.

In the world today, a man is lonely and distant. His world is a virtual world. He's lazy and blunted with cheap entertainment.

As a human race we messed up continuously. We behave like nothing touches us. We act indifferently. There is always something wrong. We blame others. We exist on urges. The world as such is going to hell. A man as a human being is helpless.

The truth is the world is a beautiful place in spite of all the contradictions. In spite of what it became. The road led me to different places where I had a feeling I had it on my palm.

And now I think about what I know. I do that when I try to put things into perspective. I close my eyes and hope for the best.

Well... it could be said that I've kind of lost interest in the whole thing. Sort of feeling I struggle with inside. Sometimes I hear it as waves engulfing a shore. A strong wind that blows. Sometimes I feel it as a season of a year.

They say you can always start from all over again. Personally, I believe in new beginnings. They could mean anything. You can think of yourself as anyone.

So what does that make it all? I'm not sure. I am not really sure about anything at this point...

Maybe I could start from the very beginning and moment when it all went... differently. I don't really know what or how to think of it. Was it the wrong timing? Was it bad luck? Maybe I would live a different life. Maybe I'd be someone else. Perhaps it all would have been different.

I am, however, not another sad story. No. I refuse to be. Who in God's name would read me? I wear a smile. Smiling is an easy act. It is beautiful and free in the world where we can choose who we want to be. As for me, I am the energy, freedom and free will. It's kinda odd for me to talk about myself because when I do, I feel like I'm talking about someone else. "There is another man in every man", someone once said. I've found that to be true.

I had a dream... in which I'm waking up on a bed in some kind of space that looks like some kind of a room. I walk to the window, look through it. It's narrow and tall... I don't know why it's like that. It is just like that in a dream. I look through it while clouds are passing by. Different shapes and forms. Dark clouds, gray ones. They are passing very closely by the window. Some of them are breaking on it, diluting, like smoke. I have never seen them up close. Well, maybe once before when I flew on the plane...

So I'm high. My consciousness lives among them. All I see looks like some kind of passing state of mind. I'm looking at the world from that distance. I focus on one part of it. I see a city. I see it like an island. I see the surface of the most famous park in the world. I walked that city's streets. I'd listened to its sounds, breathing the air... Felt kind of odd. Now I'm looking at it from here. I don't know why. That's what my dream is like. My dreams are abstract and erotic.

*

I opened my eyes and woke up with a sigh. I was lying on a side looking at emptiness in front of me. I was breathing in silence for a few moments. I had an odd feeling like I was sort of transparent. Like everything I knew was a dream in that particular moment. I dream a lot, like I said.

Then I heard a song... Radiohead - "Everything in its right place", was playing inside my mind. It was like I had a moment with that song for everything that followed.

Usually I would be awakened by my neighbor's loud so - called music or some screaming pig before slaughtering, dogs baking, nearby church bells ringing... Welcome to my neighborhood. Someone could or may find this kind of romantic but I don't know if people in this hood do. I think romance is foreign language for them.

Anyway, this morning wasn't so. A song I heard in my head reminded me of something. On a dream... no, a movie I've seen. A dream the main character had in it. A man who snowboarded his entire life surfing on high waves his way of life he inherited from his successful, rich father, not taking things seriously. He meets a girl in whom he gets in love with but ends up having an accident with another when a woman who was driving and wanted to believe he loves her, loses control while speeding, runs off the bridge and slams on a big concrete wall... He stayed alive but his face was ruined. From there everything changes for him. He goes along with a confusion of dream and reality. At the end of the movie he opens his eyes with consciousness he dreamt the whole thing. In a dream he thought he had a life he wanted. In a dream, he unconsciously controlled everything. But things went wrong and got out of control. Events took him to the very point he needed to decide. He told himself he didn't want to live in a dream. He wanted to wake up. He decided to live in the real world. He jumped from the building in his dream and opened his eyes.

And now it was like that song I heard was telling me a story. It was like it interpreted what I was feeling. What if a whole life could be a dream? When things would happen just the way we'd want them to. As if all would be like we imagine it. Maybe that would make it a very interesting dream.

I uncovered myself, got up from the bed (which is actually a mattress on the floor next to the window). I walked the room naked, going to the bathroom, coming to the mirror putting my hands on a sink. I stared at my neglected, sleepy face… Then I started to wash my face by putting soap on it. I took a razor, starting to shave. Nothing was heard except flowing water and razor going over the skin.

So after I finished shaving, I wiped myself still looking at the mirror. Skin was soft, smooth, gentle and tender, like a baby's skin. I went over the cheeks and beard with my hand. I took a look at my body. I thought about it. I was looking at it the way it was… My body was broken. Left side was a lot weaker than the right side. Right hand was longer than my left. My body was strong, healthy, and in good shape. I live believing that it's so. I wonder how I would feel if I lived in another body.

This body evolves and develops. That is its nature. From the moment it was an embryo, fetus, an image on screen in mother's womb, then it went south and little shape of life led to tough and painful fight for existence by a cause of unprofessionalism, ignorance, bad timing?

I was born broken. I was born with a nonfunctional left side. No one knew what would happen to me. No one believed I'd survive. They gave up on me. But I was strong and big. I made it. I wonder how. I wonder inside. I was in critical condition for days. They didn't let my mom see me. They didn't even keep her informed. She lost a lot of blood and strength during the labor. We were close to losing our lives. My mom lives with a totally different consciousness of it.

Life and death… How do these words sound? Do they have weight? Or are they weightless like a feather? Oftentimes I imagine myself being someone or something else. My mind becomes different. It changes its shape and form. I feel it is limitless and free. I feel it is pretty like everything I see. Strange mind, that is it is kind of funny feeling it like a mush. Feeling it like honey.

People lose their lives every single day in different ways.

Every day a life gets born. Lives are born. Every day there's a smile on someone's face. Every day someone sheds a tear. Every day this world gets to be the place for someone else while someone leaves it. I wonder where they go… so called dead ones. Wherever that is I hope it's a happy, joyful place.

I looked at a reflection of my broken body. I looked at the right side stronger than the left side. I wondered about its nature of how it works… and how it does not.

I pinch myself, it hurts. I put the muscle straight, it gets hard. Whichever part of my body I pull, it gets hard.

I looked at my face in the mirror… getting closer to it slowly. It's totally quiet.

"I feel sick…", it was like I could hear the reflection. "It's tight…it's dark. I want to get out. Why are you looking at me like that? How do you feel like somebody who stands there and stares in his own reflection? You know who I am. You are conscious more than you want to be indifferent. You act cold. You look at yourself, you see me… I'm a feeling of desire. A craving. An extreme. I'm conscious. I'm your disheveled messy hair, overgrown bird. I'm an act. I'm an action. I am someone who you become when you think of somebody else you'd be. I'm a voice and a pain in your head. I'm all restless. Pain which strangles you inside. I'm your bloodstream. I'm your different thoughts. Someone who you talk to. I'm a whisper. I'm dancing. Seducing… I'm your dick while it gets hard. I am fucking. I'm your limb's head. A loud motor sound. I'm a force of power. I am salvation. I'm everything, everywhere."

I was just standing there, looking at it distantly in silence.

"You are not gonna say anything? You're not gonna do anything? You think too much. You are slow and boring. Tell me… what would you do if you were rich? So fucking rich… you could afford anything. If you could do whatever you want. Can you imagine yourself in that situation? Can you picture yourself in that role? It confuses you, it turns me on. You think of yourself not being materialistic in the material world. Are you really what you think you are? Or you're ignoring a thought you are creasy. You're a funny guy, you know that? God I need a cigarette…"

I felt cold. I heard the sound of a mower from outside. I needed coffee.

I looked away at the shattered particles of dust looking like they were snow in the air, on a bright, morning sunray shining through my window. I imagined being like those particles. I was in a way. They were like floating on air from my clothes, out of my hair. From a towel I wiped myself with. They looked so light and simply beautiful, white, gleaming particles of dust.

I put my clothes on, and walked the space going downstairs. Nobody's around. I could still hear the mower motor sound. I anticipated it to go off. I like silence. But it didn't.

I opened the kitchen closet, took a cup putting water in a cattle, setting it on a stove flames. I leaned on a shelf staring in water. I looked at it while it started bubbling. I put it off, puttin' coffee in it. A smell and taste have an effect like elixir, a potion that does its thing.

Then I noticed something. I didn't hear the mower any more. It was perfectly quiet and peaceful again. I took a cup of coffee and I walked out on a terrace. I leaned on the old, wooden fence. Day was pretty. Sun was shining. I took a sip of coffee and looked at the sky. Vanilla colored clouds. It's winter. It's funny how weather can affect people's mood. We talk about the weather all the time. How it was, how it is, how it is going to be. Some people talk about it like their very life depends on it. And then all different weather happens. People lose their homes, their lives. They lose each other. They lose their pets. They end up on the street with no one and nothing. Just like that. And you realize what they were talking about. What they were afraid of. Or it passes as news for you for that day. That moment while you hear about it until you start hearing about something else.

It's a nice day. Things were looking like something nice and interesting could happen.

I drank my coffee and looked around. I had noticed my father mowing the lawn. He was standing on fresh, mowed grass in peace and quiet. He was smoking his cigarette. He looked distant. He was having a break before he moved on. He didn't notice me.

I turned my head towards the sun and it wormed my face. All of a sudden I felt sort of a headache. I heard a clownish laughter of that reflection I saw in a mirror earlier. I could see it now angry and aggressive. He made a sudden move slamming and breaking a glass with his head.

He slowly moved back looking at me like he hated me while the blood went slowly down his forehead.

I closed my eyes trying to massage my forehead.

I took my coffee looking at what I saw. I felt grateful for this big place with a big garden. It looked good. Well, it looked good to me. I could be there whenever I wanted. Like, now, for example.

I've been here for a while. In this big, family house, for months with no electricity, sometimes no water (which is polluted anyway). I sleep on a mattress wearing a winter coat covered with two blankets, grateful for every meal. Grateful for anything edible I can put in my mouth, eat and swallow. No job, no idea. Trying to figure out what's next…

But I kind of feel optimistic somehow. I don't know. I guess it's in my nature. Maybe I could call it a form of religion. Although life at this place is pure survival in every possible way. People work their way through it. They are reduced to doing all kinds of things to survive. That is everyday life.

I watch those people. They look distant. They look like they don't care. They look creasy.

So I think about the things I believe. About things I want to believe…

What does it really mean believing in something? Personally I don't belong to any religion. My parents did a good thing by not christening me. They wanted me to find it for myself.

It used to be food. I was passionate and ambitious about it. I was trying to be creative. We started a modest, family business. I was excited and grateful about it. That business had its ups and downs. It's interesting how you can find ways to grow business out of basic human needs. Or should I say needs of every living thing. It all started with hunger. Nowadays it's a business of playing with innovations for modern society. All kinds of people are doing it now. People are poor and hungry. Maybe someone is dying of hunger right now because he or she can't afford it. People do all kinds of things for a meal. I can't help but ask myself every time I get hungry. Humans became greedy. Money is part of every conversation in society of consumers. Every day someone is born and somebody dies in that world. Someone's life and death doesn't mean anything except what it is. We lose ourselves in it. We neglect our own identity, reducing it to money, instant pleasures and superficiality.

What happens when we ask ourselves what our purpose is? When we forget and don't even try. When we shut off from everything 'cause something hurts or causes pain. What happens when we don't care and act indifferently?

Life is too short to have limits. It is all too short for anything to be imposed. Life came about free with consciousness and free will. Life is independent. It connects. That is how its nature is. Life evolves.

I was sitting on a concrete terrace still having my coffee. I looked at the garden, I looked at all the green around. I looked at the trees. Nobody likes winter, although, this one is in passing. Wind blew through treetops shaking them strongly.

And then, for some reason, I thought about the moment I was somewhere else sitting at the dock next to the concrete path that led all the way around the Slovenian coast. I lived and worked there for years. Sun was going down leaving colors in the sky. It was quite a sight, beautiful and simple. I was trying to imagine more beautiful things looking for comfort, trying to survive. It was peaceful and quiet. Darkness was falling slowly. There was the sound of the sea and birds. Different lights on buildings in the distance were turning on.

I stood up after a while, started walking the path. I looked at the sight in the sky. I looked at the wide, distant sea, having some kind of a healing effect. I felt my mind free, like it widened.

I heard the others. I hear the street, the noise. All kinds of different lights shone. I pulled out my IPOd from my pocket, putting headphones in my ears.

Previous night I was coming back from work. I was serving dinner in a hotel I worked in. I walked in the dark to my room where I was staying. My roommate, Johny, who was a company scholar and who did all kinds of things for hotel resorts, came along and shone a light on me.

"Hey, your room is open," he said in Slovenian.

"Open?" I said.

"Yea, your door is open."

He shone on the closed curtain. Door was broken, semi closed. It was breaking and entering. Someone had a system. So I slowly pushed the door and went in. I took a few steps in the dark inside, having a feeling what happened. I turned on the light and saw a mess. Room was in chaos.

Things were everywhere. Closet was open and in a mess. In a moment I knew what was missing. A backpack I had and all in it. Everything I had. Somebody was quick. That was the second attempt of breaking. The one before happened a few weeks earlier. Somebody was noticed and ran off. He tried again and made it. Good for him.

I walked out while my roommate was, by getting the situation, talking about something I didn't hear. I stood next to the broken door with my hands in my pockets, looking at the stars of the bright sky. I slowly took the breath in and out. At that moment I didn't, couldn't think of anything but the book I was trying to publish. It was there, in a computer, in a backpack. I digested a feeling I was left without. In a moment I felt I was falling from high. I felt like that was everything I knew. I felt lost. Dark and empty. I felt ridiculous, all because of a book. Written words…

I went back to my room, sat on the bed and laid on it. I stared at the ceiling powerless to think about anything. I closed my eyes and fell asleep.

Chapter 2

Road took me home and now I was sitting on a step, looking at what's around. Looking at my neighborhood thinking about what's next. I was looking at people here and I thought about how they live although I didn't know them. They are freezing on streets, in their homes, looking for any kind of shelter. They go to churches to warm themselves sitting in silence.

Nobody knows what's going to happen. I remember a conversation between a couple of us. Someone had said it won't be a third world war but such an economic crisis, social collapse and poverty. And yet the Earth keeps turning like nothing can stop it. I wonder for how long.

I walked back inside, walked through the house into my room. I came close to the window. I looked at the neighborhood. A horizon of houses and trees sun shined on. I looked at the houses' roofs red in the sun. It was so quiet and passive. I felt so distant here. So far away.

Then I felt like I'd take a walk. I don't go out during the day except when I need to. But now I felt I'd do it. I took my music, walked out through my backyard and saw the dog walking in his box. Big, black Rottweiler's name was Paw. I remember when he was brought into our home. He was a puppy. He was smaller than his head looked right now. He looked sleepy. He looked sleepy most of the time I saw him. He's old. There's white slime in the corners of his eyes. He looked at me with tender, tired, old eyes… I reached my hand and cuddled him. He closed his eyes looking like he liked that. He sniffed my hand and licked it. He did what dogs do. I tried to clean his eyes. He looked like it didn't bother him. I took a part of it with my longest finger looking at it. Paw looked at me like he wondered what I was doing. He sniffed me and licked me slowly and gently. I was thinking of taking him for a walk but I didn't want to put a leash on him. I didn't want to tie him. I opened the box door and let him out. Paw was not my dog. He was my brother's dog. Brother got married and moved. Paw had his house and space in his box. He was considered a family member. Now he was loosened I looked at him running happily and free. So I left him at that. Paw is dead now. He is buried under a tree in the garden. Rest his soul.

I walked out on the street. Day was fine. There's no one around. I walked the street aimlessly with my hands in my pockets. I saw a gravel stone as I walked. I kicked it while watching it roll somewhere…

I'm a man walking. I walk everywhere.

So what could I tell you about? I could tell you about… this place I live in, a little city in Serbia, called Zrenjanin. I was born here. I grew up here. But I'm not really sure what I feel about it. Every place on this planet has its own identity. A story.

It was slowly getting dark. Night is a specific time for me. At night things seem different. At night I have a feeling my mind is widening, setting free to wander. My consciousness becomes different. As a kid I thought night time was a time when miracles happen. I was a dreamer. Still am.

I walked the street, distant… with music playing in my ears. A woman's voice sang a song. It was a slow song. It sounded suitable as I walked along. A woman that sang was someone I knew personally. She had a band with whom she played in clubs. One time, we talked about music when she told me she'd send me a song she sang on to listen to the sound of her voice and piano. So I was listening to it while I walked. It felt good on that particular winter day.

I was crossing over the bridge under which a river flew. I always think of a story from long ago when people used to make soups using water from this river. Now it's polluted. It has been for a very long time. It boils from every poison you can think of.

Then I noticed someone walking, getting closer to the corner, nearby, calling me.

It was my best friend.

"Hey man, what's up?" he asked.

"Nothing…" I said.

"You look terrible," he said smiling.

"Don't ask."

"Come on. Let's go for a beer."

"I don't have any money."

"It's ok. I got it."

I have a few best friends. Knowing them I realized what it means to have a friend. Whether you know them your entire life or just met them.

My friend likes to walk too. So we walked. We went downtown. There was nothing there but a few people walking, passing by. It seemed sad. My friend bought us a beer and we went to the lake, our favorite part of the city. We came to a bench, sat down. We'd go there every time we'd hangout.

"So what's up? How are you?" he said while opening the can and having some.

"I'm fucking fantastic," I said looking at the lake.

He looked at me. "Self-loathing, really?"

I took a long breath in and out…

"How's a novel going?"

"I don't know…"

We were drinking beer in silence, looking at the lake. There were a couple of swans floating. We looked at the city looking like a postcard from there. Cold beer flew through our thoughts.

"This place is home," I said. "I just have to figure it out."

My friend looked at me.

"Sure… how is that working out for you?"

"Like you have just stepped on my toe", I said while having a sip.

"Funny… Good thing you didn't lose a sense of humor."

"Well, it can happen any time now."

We smiled and had some beer. We sat in silence. Air was fresh, and the beer was tasty. The little bar across the lake was playing some music. I meditated on that.

I was traveling for years but didn't stay anywhere long. Now I am stuck here with no actual idea about what is next. I had no job, no life. My perspective was shaken. I was lost. I needed to do something. I needed to be cool about it.

"So what do you wanna do tonight?" my friend asked me.

"I don't know."

"You wanna see a movie, see a show?"

I looked at my beer can, wandered off somewhere. I looked at the color of the sky. Then I drank some more beer.

"Let's go for a show," I said.

We walked some more, and went to the city theater. I practically grew up in that theater, having my mom work there as a puppeteer. It was kind of saving me from what could harm me. I could have ended up on that stage. Well…that is a whole other story.

After the show we went to a bar. The same one playing music while we were having beer on benches. Bar had a terrace very close to a lake. That was the only thing worth it. It was Sunday, a day for live jam sessions. I didn't know about them but one night a friend of mine took me and now I kind of wait every Sunday to hear them.

There weren't many people, my friend got lost somewhere while I listened to the music, drinking my beer.

After a while I took my beer and walked out. Fresh, night air was cold and felt good. I could breathe. I looked at the lake and the night sky.

"Hey man, what happened? Where did you go?" my friend said.

"I wanted some fresh air."

"Are you ok?" he said.

"I guess… You?"

"Yea you wanna get out of here?"

"I don't know…" I shrugged my shoulders.

"Come on. Let's go." He said.

We went to a pub and again I found myself with a bottle of beer in my hand. I bored my ass off. I looked at people, always the same. I looked at the faces I wasn't interested in. But the music was good. Time was passing.

I went out. There was a table there. I stood there, holding beer, looking at the street, looking at people coming and going. The hours were late and people were drunk. They were going out singing loud, waving with their drinks having what they called good times for themselves.

At some point I saw some two girls standing not far away from me. Some of the gays I knew were talking to them. My friend was one of them. I looked at them feeling totally insignificant. Yet I wanted them both. It was like this urge to do something terrible I felt inside. I was thinking about that feeling which was that reflection in a mirror I saw that morning. I felt like a clown. Like a monster. I was bored to death.

Next thing I knew was I was somehow closer to them. My friend looked at me and smiled.

"Now this guy... you gotta meet," my friend said.

I felt shame and pain but excitement too. I didn't want to talk to them 'cause the talk was always the same. But then I felt something. I felt some kind of... life inside. I felt hot. I started to sweat. I was talking and talking. Everybody was laughing. We kept talking while dawn was slowly coming.

We walked girls home telling them we'll see each other again.

We walked home the quiet, empty streets in silence, looking at the colors of dawn. It was like the whole world was sleeping. Morning light was widening in the sky. Stray dogs were walking around.

"There's something fuzzy about this picture," I said.

"What do you mean?" my friend said, looking at me.

"Do you feel that?"

"What?"

"Total and otter peace."

"Oh peace is it?"

"You don't think it is?"

My friend started to laugh. "Ah peace...You gotta appreciate it. Peace is like... music. It can be beautiful, it can be disturbing. You create it, you choose it. You are setting the tone. At this hour you can call it however you want."

We kept walking. Streetlights were changing colors.

"You wanna go for a cup of coffee?"

"Ok." I said.

We went for coffee. It was a sunny morning so we sat outside.

"It all seems simple from this perspective," my friend said.

"What do you mean?"

"Well the night we just had. Sitting here having coffee."

"It's called relaxing," I said, smiling.

My friend put his sunglasses on fixing a chair he was sitting on like he was going for a nap. I looked around. Sun was shining. People were walking, coming and going, having their everyday life. I was slowly starting to get sleepy. I had some coffee, looking around.

Then, for some reason, I noticed someone who was coming our way. It looked like a man. He had a long coat and a hat. He walked among other people. There was something about him. Something familiar about his appearance. He was getting closer. He walked right at us.

"Mind if I join you?" he said.

My friend looked at him over his sunglasses.

"Feel free."

"Thank you," Man said. He pulled up a chair and sat down. "How's it going?"

"Ok…" my friend said. "And you are?"

"Me? Well let's ask this guy…" a Man said mildly smiling, looking at me.

My friend looked at me, looking a bit taken.

"Who would I be, hmm? What do you think?" I looked at the man wordlessly.

"What if I tell you how all is going to play out? How is everything going to happen? What the rest of your life is going to look like."

I kept looking at him.

"What do you think?" Man said, looking at me. "What if I tell you how you are going to die. Would you really want to know? What if I say I'm God himself? You look at all these people. You think about them. Think about their lives. What does it all mean? You think about the life you want to have. You think about what it takes."

"What is this? Who are you?"My friend had said .

"Tell you what…" Man said. He pulled out a piece of paper and a pen and wrote something on it.

"Here… Come and find me. We should talk."

Then he just got up, put the chair back, looked at us and simply walked away.

I took a piece of paper and looked at it. It looked like some kind of a map. He marked a place on it. I looked at my friend. He looked at me.

"Well that was weird," he said.

I turned around looking at a man walking away. I took a look at the map.

"This is going to sound kinda creasy," I said.

My friend looked at me.

"What if somehow… he is that Man?"

"What Man?"

"A Man… you drew."

"What?"

I looked at him.

My friend started to laugh.

"Man, you need to get some sleep. You're losing your mind."

I looked at the map…

"You realize what you are saying… " he said.

"Just a funny feeling…"

"A funny feeling…" he said. "So a Man who we just had a weird chat with on the street is the same someone I made a sketch of on paper? Is that it?"

I folded a piece of paper with a map on and put it in my pocket while my friend watched me. We had coffee and headed home. Although I didn't want to go home. I thought about the man on my way back. I thought about a map he gave me. It was kind of odd. I mean who this man was. Well let me tell you about him.

Chapter 3

It was some time ago…

I was in my room in the darkness, having an odd night. Or should I say I struggled with a strange feeling inside. I was working on one of my stories. Well… I was trying to work. TV was on but I didn't really watch it. I sat on the floor and started going through a book I took. I looked through the window at a clear, bright, night sky. I was in some kind of a moment. I felt distant. Like out there, among stars. I felt some kind of presence inside. I stared at the floor. I looked at the TV screen. I saw many people walking. Then I heard music playing. For some reason I imagined someone walking in my mind. I started following him.. My mind ran on its motion. I felt it was some sort of odd spirit. So I had a feeling about this person. I tried to see who he would be. I saw him walking. But that was all. So I decided to name him "Man walking", for whatever comes and he does next. So I thought about him ever since.

I told my friend what happened. I described it all to him and told him how I imagined he'd look and be like. My friend is an artist so one day he made a sketch of him (I wanted to do it but I am terrible at drawing). I had an idea… more like a need to write about him although I didn't know anything about him. So I couldn't tell you who this person really is as well as where he came from. And he appeared now…as odd as that may be.

I came home later that day and looked for the sketch. I rummaged through my stuff and finally found it. I just looked at it. And then I looked through the window. I put the sketch and piece of paper with a map on the table. I didn't know what to think. I just looked at it.

Then I heard the sound of a bell ringing. It was coming from a monastery not far away. I could see it from my room window. I got up and walked to the window. I looked at the scenery while I still heard it.

"It's so fucking boring…"

I turned around and saw myself at the other side of the room.

"Let's do something. Let's go somewhere."

I turned back, kept looking through the window.

"Do you hear me?"

"Yes I hear you," I said. "We can't afford anything."

"Well what the fuck are you gonna do about it? When was the last time you got laid?"

"Shut up. You are just a voice in my head."

"And you are fucking voice in mine. I can't believe we are the same person. You are like fucking bad taste in my mouth."

He grinned at me pulling his tongue out.

"And you are the bad taste in mine."

He smiled sadly at me, putting his head between his hands.

"I wish I could burst out of your chest like an alien or something."

"That's funny. I feel you like one."

"You are fucking killing me…"

"What do you want from me?"

"Things I want…"

He took a deep breath in and out.

"Right now… I wish for a smoke."

"Those things kill."

"Is that you being funny? Wow… didn't know you have it in you. What else do you have?"

"Why are you such a prick?"

"It's a gift. You wanna do something?"

"Yeah I kinda do. I wanna punch you in the face."

He started laughing.

"You wanna play a tough guy? Bring it on."

I pushed him, he slammed on the wall. He punched me, and I fell on the floor. We grabbed one another and started pulling, pushing, punching… We fell on the floor, rolling. His face was bloody. So was mine. We grabbed each other's thoughts and started falling on the stairs.

I slammed on the floor hitting my head. I heard buzzing in my ears. I had a terrible headache. I couldn't move… and then I could. I tried to get up slowly. I went to the bathroom and washed my face. I felt anger and pain. I felt ridiculous. I walked around the house thinking what to do.

I decided to go for it. I decided to find him. I just packed my stuff. Well actually I didn't need anything except my music, some food and water. I was on my way. I hit the road. I looked for the way the map was taking me.

I came to somewhere that looked like a long path leading to what looked like woods. So there I was, walking among trees, feeling kind of odd. I didn't really know what I was doing. Being at this place I felt like I could forget about everything else. I felt kind of free. I felt empty. I kept walking, following a lead. I felt something evolving inside. So after a while of walking, I felt like I could find God himself. Woods was a huge and amazing place.

So after losing sense of direction, time and really everything else… I'd found myself on some cliff. Water was falling, sounding smooth. I looked at the breathtaking scenery. I felt totally lost but found it at the same time. I was fine. I moved on. I went along the way some rivers flew, and found some food on the way.

After I didn't know how long I was walking, I saw someone on a little shore. I came closer, trying to make as little noise as I could. He was sitting, holding a fishing rod. It was peaceful and quiet.

"So you've found your way how to come I see…" he said.

"What are you doing here?"I said.

"What do you mean?"

I looked at him.

"Well… I live here."

He swung his wooden stick.

"You're probably asking yourself about who I am…" he said."Take a look around. Do you like this place? Do you like what you see? Where exactly do you think you are?"

"I have no idea."

"Well…That's why I'm here. I am here because you need me."

"How's that?"

"We could be anywhere and yet we are here. Why do you think that is?"

I looked at him.

"We are kind of like how this river flows," he said. "Tell me... Why did you really come?"

"I… can't even begin to..."

"It's ok," he said "You can always start from somewhere."

"Let's start from you," I said.

"Ok, well... I guess we have a job to do. Do you know how to catch a fish?"

I looked at the river.

"Here," he said, giving me a rod. "Try it. Let's see if you can catch our dinner. This river is a mystery. It holds a secret. You never know what you're gonna get."

Water looked crystal clear. Sun rays sparkled on it. It looked pure and magical. I wasn't much of a fisherman (I wasn't a fisherman at all) but I gave it a shot. So at some point, something started to bite. I have never killed anything in my life (except a few insects) and here I was, killing this fish. Man looked at me, smiling mildly.

"You got a good one there," he said encouriging me.

We made dinner out of it while the sun went down. We ate in silence. I felt like I could spend the rest of my days at that place. My mind was clear. I felt no pain, just curiosity. This place looked simple.

Man took me to his house in the middle of, well... nowhere. It was a small, wooden house. He made us tea.

"So tell me," he said while pouring us tea.

I looked at it while it smoked out of the cup.

"I don't know how to talk about it…"

"Just start from somewhere. Anywhere."

"I kind of lost interest in the whole thing."

"Lost interest?"

I had some tea.

"Why do you think that is?" Man said.

"Don't know... just is."

"It sounds worse than it is... Well you know what they say about how you can always start from somewhere, in your case from this very place."

I looked at him.

"You started a new novel. That's something too."

"I don't quite know what I'm doing."

"You're doing what you like. You are doing what you meant to do. The thing you're good at. You came to this place you want to be and… you are taking a leap of faith with me. I am real, you know. I know it's strange."

"So what did you mean by me needing you?" I said.

"Well…everybody needs somebody. People are lonely. This world is running broken. There is no easy way out. You get along with that or get away from that. That is your choice. The question is… what makes you make it. And more importantly, what do you really want? How badly do you want it?"

I had some tea.

"You've been to places. You've seen stuff," Man said. "Now you are here. But I can't help you if you don't help yourself. You know what dancing is? You remember how you love to dance? This world is a playground. A stage. We need to figure out what is the next step for you…tomorrow. I'm off to bed."

I took some tea, slowly stood up and walked to the door. I could smell the woods. I listened to it. It was dark. But the sky was bright. I looked at the stars hoping for something they'd tell me. Anything… Well, maybe not… but there was this feeling inside. Like inside gravitation. But I didn't know what to do with it exactly. I struggled with it.

Well… there wasn't much else to do there so I went to bed too. I tried to think but with every thought I got more tired. So much so, that I shacked. That was the last thing I remember before I couldn't tell any more about what was dream and what was reality.

Chapter 4

Iwoke up the next day with that clown-face reflection scaring me, getting into my face. I took a breath of life into me. Morning was sunny and warm. Bright sunlight shone through the windows. I smelled fresh coffee. Man came from somewhere outside holding bags in his hands.

"Good morning," he said. "How did you sleep?"

"Ok I guess..."

"I brought you some food. Good stuff."

"Thank you. So how long have you been here?"

"A while. Here... have some fresh fruit and coffee."

I had some coffee.

"We are going for a trip," he said.

"A trip? What kind of trip?"

"A boat trip. Weather is good."

"You have a boat too?"

"I made it. Let's go."

We walked through the woods in silence. It was like it was alive. We came to shore, walked into the boat and set off.

"I'm taking you to see where you are," he said.

So we paddled. It all looked pretty impressive. Like land lost in time.

"So where have you been before you came here?"

Man looked at me. "Everywhere but this is not about me. It's about you."

"What are we doing?"

"You'll see. You came here looking for answers. I'm here to help you."

"Who does that make you?"

"Does it really matter?"

"I want to hear more."

"There is time for more. Try to relax. You think too much."

"Is that a bad thing?"

"There isn't just yes or no answer."

I looked at him

Man smiled.

"Did I say something funny?"

"Take a look around. This…is all you. What you see is what you know."

"Why do I have the feeling it's a trick of some kind?"

"You are an imaginative person. You tell me."

Man looked at me and paddled.

"Do you believe in God?" he said.

"Is that a trick question?"

"It's a simple question."

"You told me I could consider you as God."

"Is that a yes?"

"I believe by questioning."

"How is that working out for you?"

"You tell me. I want you to do the talking."

"It is simple really. But I can't make you a believer. You can make yourself a believer."

We paddled on wide water surrounded by woods, mountains and cliffs.

"We are going to make a stop here," Man said. "We'll have lunch. I want you to meet someone."

We dragged a boat on shore and started walking through more woods.

We got close to a place where we saw someone working around the house. It was a man with short, gray hair, gray beard. He looked like he had trouble walking.

"Hey Gary," Man said. "How's it going?"

Gary turned and looked at us, blinking from the sunlight getting into his eyes.

"Fine, just fine…" he said. "What's going on?"

"I want you to meet my friend."

Gary started to clean his dirty hands on his clothes.

Mark, Gary, we shook hands.

"How about lunch?" the man said.

"All right..." Gary said.

We made a grill. Had some barbecue, ate in peace.

"Gary here...has a story,"Man said. "Isn't that right Gary?"

Gary was chewing food in his mouth.

"He has spent thirty years in prison. He was locked with killers, rapists, sex offenders, psychopaths, all kinds of criminals. He lived like a homeless man. He has skills... Don't you Gary? Everything he knows he learned in prison. He's a mechanic. He can fix anything. He's good with cards."

Gary took a Bible in his hands and started tearing pages. He took tobacco, started rolling. His hands and clothes were neglected and dirty from work. He lit a cigar pulling a smoke, inhaling wisdom, as he'd call it.

"He came here to spend his days, to feel useful. Away from everybody and everything."

Gary took a smoke, then took a deck of cards from his pocket. He started mixing them...

"The thing I've learned in prison... is weakness makes you stronger. There is no secret. The secret is what this place really holds. That is why I came here. Tricks, on the other hand, are all around us. They are everywhere, starting from here..." Gary pointed to his head. He took a smoke, mixed the cards laying them on the little table.

"Hmm..." he mumbled, breathing smoke out. "You are a searcher... You live your life in different places. But you are out of focus. Your mind and soul are among stars. You travel looking for a home of your own. Your story is your journey. The thing that led you here is a spirit that wanders. The question is... what is the thing you are looking to find at this place."

He took a long smoke looking at me." What do you think that is?"

I looked at him. "You see all that in cards?"

"Sure..." he said. " They have a funny way of showing things.

We looked at one another. I looked at the Man. Then I took some food and I started chewing... thinking whether these two are even real.

We sat in peace and quiet, eating food.

"So what else do you see?" I said.

Gary took a big, long, slow smoke."Well…it looks like a puzzle. It is a puzzle. Like the thing you'd have to figure out inside whatever brought you here. The hardest struggle is the struggle inside."

I looked at the man.

"You are drawn by distances…" Gary went on. "You feel them like everything and nothing. You walk towards those distances in your mind but you never quite get there, although, you feel like you are closer every time. So you keep walking and walking and after a while you just walk with this feeling inside you don't quite know where you are. You fight that feeling 'cause that's how your nature is like. Although, you feel like you are on the verge of giving up. You feel it strong, you fight, getting numb to the point you feel the power of rising and overcoming your biggest enemy, yourself. That's your struggle. That is the art within you. You get empowered by it. You get oddly conscious of it. That's your element, the battle inside."

Gary was talking, opening the cards, laying them on the table.

"Are you buying this?" Man said, looking at me.

I looked at him.

"These are not just any cards, you know?" he said." These are HIS cards. It is really up to you what is going to happen next."

He looked at me.

"Choices," he said.

I felt strange. I felt like I was everywhere and nowhere at the same time. I felt like falling in an endless, big, black hole.

It was slowly getting dark. Gary lit up the fire. We sat around it looking at the fire burning peacefully, having some drink Gary made out from herbs.

"What are you thinking?" Man asked me at some point.

I shook my head. "I feel like being present and absent at the same time."

"Is that a good thing or bad thing?"

"I don't know. It just is."

Fire was cracking, picturing woods around us. Gary looked like he was sleeping.

"You've told me you could tell me what the rest of my life looks like. How I die, that I can consider you as God himself."

Man looked at me.

"What does that mean? Who are you? Where do you come from?"

Man looked at the burning fire.

"I am present, like you are. And absent, like you get. You are a creative person, imaginative. It doesn't really matter where I come from. What matters is that I am here. You really want me to tell you the rest of your life… You want to know as much as you don't. You are giving it a lot of thinking 'cause you're at a peculiar time and place of telling what is and what isn't. The unpredictability, fight for existence. It doesn't end, you know. Even if I tell you, would you really believe me? Would you take it seriously? What would you do about it? You think your life would be easier? Take a look around. Go ahead. Look up. Tell me what you see."

I looked up. Night sky was clear and bright.

"Tell me what you see."

"I see a sky full of stars."

"God is all that and more. Much more," Man said. "You don't buy it. I can tell," he said looking at me. "That's all right. He's misunderstood. Everybody's looking for an explanation, clarification. It's easier to believe in what you see and feel. It all comes from the mind. All creation. His existence is unfathomable. Like the universe is unbelievable and endless."

"What about destruction? What about pain and suffering? What is that?"

"Pain is part of life. If pain and suffering is the only thing u see…you won't be able to see anything else. Like that thing inside you fight with. You feel it strongly, you feel like you're on the verge of giving up. You fight, get numb to the point you feel the power of rising and overcoming your biggest enemy, yourself. Your mind is like this sky above us. It's like a garden. A big, good looking, beautiful garden. It is really up to you how you perceive it. It is up to you what it looks like. It's the same with the world. The word is beautiful."

"And then, bad things happen."

"Things happen… that have nothing to do with the world," Man said. "You call them bad or good…"

"What would you call them?"

"I wouldn't call them at all."

"What does that mean?"

"Do you believe in heaven and hell? Like the actual places?"

I looked at him. "Is that another trick question?"

"It's strange to think about existence outside of this word. Life, gods, what is, what isn't. You hear stories but you don't know what to make of it really. And then, things happen to you. All kinds of different things you try to make sense of what the world is. There is no suitable answer. There is no answer you get satisfied with. World is not black and white. I would say that's the primordial state of your struggle."

I looked at him.

"Everything is connected amazingly. We are just not aware of that or neglecting it for whatever reason."

I took a sip of whatever Gary made, looking at the fire.

Man looked at me

"What is happiness for you?" he said.

"What?"

"What makes you happy?"

I looked at him. "Seriously?"

"Seriously."

"Do you believe in happiness?"

I hesitated slightly, smiling.

"Did I say something funny?"

"It's… a state of mind, really."

"A state of mind…ok, what is your mind telling you now?"

"It's odd. like I'm far inside."

"That's because you are hiding. You don't let yourself be seen. You don't like to be exposed. That way you can be yourself. Where does that state of mind come from?"

"It's an impression."

"Very good. What happens to it?"

"It is… the feeling that means we are humans."

"Go on."

"The time of now is the only time there is. We choose how happy we are and how happy we get."

"You feel far inside being at this place. Anything can change at any time. How do you consider what has happened to you?"

"It's… hard for me to talk about anything at this point."

"I'll help you through it. Tell me."

"I live in a broken body in a broken, senseless world. I don't trust it. I don't believe in it."

"Why is that?"

"I just don't see the point."

"A point… World evolves… like we do as our impression of it. Things change. That's the nature of it. It's not a flat line. It is not black and white. You know that."

"It's personal."

"I know. That's because you are a person. Not some animal. Do you remember how you like to dance? Remember dancing? Passion? Excitement? That's life. That energy and drive you feel inside. Remember what love feels like. Remember when you feel like you simply don't have to know anything else. That's the existence."

I bend my head through my hair with my hand. I felt weak.

"Your spirit resists I see," Man said. "I can feel it. It's ok. You'll find the way. That is why we are here. You need to be strong. I know you are. You are in a peculiar state… That is how I came to be. And here we are at this place trying to figure this out. And we will. Free your mind and see what happens. See what it feels like. Your mind is what you make of it."

The fire was cracking romantically, in silence. We lost track of time… and everything else, really. Not that it mattered at that place. Nothing mattered at this place. We kept talking. It seemed unreal and strange to me. It seemed like I may not remember any of this whenever I wake up. I liberated myself of any thoughts and concerns and felt like just being there in the present. Present was all I had.

At some point, I guess, I must have fallen asleep.

I walked in the dark. I walked down some street. No one was around. No one is ever around. No, it's in the middle of the desert. I don't see anything but the horizon of sand and black sky. So I walked… and all of sudden I noticed some building. The building was a big mall, the biggest mall in the world. I walked in, walked around. Place was crowded with people. A lot of people make noise doing whatever people do. This mall had many floors and people were everywhere. I was thinking how I ended up there? I don't care about malls. Don't like crowds, yet there I was. So I kept walking, looking around at stuff I couldn't care less about.

I was going on floors, looking at things. I was looking at different people trying to imagine what they are about. They looked differently into all different kinds of styles, living in a strange world. They looked like they were controlled and pointed by someone or something else. They looked like ants, moving around.

After a while, I got hungry. There was a whole floor of food. I looked at all kinds of different food. Some of it looked like something I would never put inside of my mouth. I'd found some good pizza and looked for a quiet place to sit and eat in peace. While eating, I'd noticed some bald, black man in one of the stores, dressed in a suit, playing saxophone. That was interesting to see and hear. He was playing his music, attracting people as they were coming and going. Music is a beautiful thing. Music is a part of our nature. We make and react to different kinds of sounds. I watched that man playing while I was eating. Food tasted better too. It was like my senses sharpened. I looked around, looked at others. I looked outside. My mind started to wander. I looked at people in their everyday lives. They looked like they weren't present… constantly looking and talking on their phones. They didn't notice anyone nor anything else. Like the world didn't exist except for what they were doing. I saw some of them eating. Putting and shuffling food in their mouth without thinking about it at all. This was their everyday life and it was all about them. They looked so boring and insignificant. Like anything could happen to them at any given moment without seeing it coming. There were all these…things around they were led by at every step on the way. Our lives were determined by things, possessions and money. At every step of the way we are pointed onto what and how our life should, can and supposed to be and look like, each and every point of it. From our birth, till our death we are told what to believe, what to think, what to feel… We go to school to learn things. We go to church to listen to God. We are surrounded by models of how we are supposed to look, what to wear… what to eat, things to spend money on. Life is created for us. We are tricked by feelings of comfort. We made a whole thing about ourselves. We'd lost our identity and lost our way.

So what was all this then, I thought… looking at those people? I noticed posters on some store windows. A good looking woman was dressed in some lingerie she advertised. She was a model and actress, looking attractive and seductive, calling out with her eyes. Well... anybody who sees this kind of thing wishes to do something to her or themselves. That's a natural urge. That's how we are. Sexuality is a pretty intimate and sometimes confusing thing. In the world of today, everything is out there to be seen. There is no privacy, nothing is sacred. We have neglected things that make us humans. We are enslaved, living our lives like sheeps, waiting for tomorrow to be different. We are strange and funny that way.

I sat still looking at that poster woman. I looked at the other stuff on sale people may have wished for to become attractive to somebody else. We are funny that way too. All the things we do for somebody else to like us. That is, I guess, another part of our nature. It's just the way it is. That was the message that the woman on the poster was showing. The attraction is a mysterious thing. Kind of devilish. It's like hunger. We can't really do nothing about it but indulge it. Whatever the thing we see we like, we wish for it. The longer I looked at the woman on the poster, the more I started to fantasize. I felt it like... basic, carnal desire. In my fantasy I drove some old-fashioned-classic car very fast on an open highway while making love to this woman which I'd never done before. It was just an image in my mind. It wasn't real. I didn't feel anything. It was a sexual illusion. I went a little further...started touching myself. Nothing. Not even the heartbeat. Then I started looking at females around. They looked alive but felt the same as an illusion. I kept looking... waiting. Then I thought about the point of me being there in the first place. The feeling was odd. I felt it like some kind of an evil spirit. It was like everything started to fade. It was like I was losing sense of myself... I was sweating, getting cold. I felt nothing. I felt my mind getting empty. My senses were fading. I was getting weakened by this... whatever this was. I was powerless over it. Food didn't taste like food any more. I was getting unable to think, to love, to care. My senses had gotten flat lined. I felt like I was losing my mind. I felt pain. My muscles were cramped. I had a terrible headache. I felt pain in my spine widening through my entire body. What in hell was this? I closed my eyes in a cramp suffering from this state. I heard some music playing. It wasn't the man with a saxophone. I heard it from somewhere inside getting louder. I felt like some kind of madness somehow. It was severe and extreme. I felt strangely led by this. Music sounded heavy, like all the pain I felt. I tried to stand up and walk to the nearest toilet. I went in, walked in one of the cabins like all broken. I fell on my knees and started vomiting. I felt something forcing my whole guts out. I was shaking, I was cold in a lot of pain, weakened…and after a while just closed my eyes meditating on this…

After…I don't know how long, I managed to get up, stand on my feet. I got out of the cabin, came to the sink strangely conscious of what I was doing. I looked at myself in the mirror, I was in a mess. I opened the water running, washed my face having a feeling I was doing this to someone else.

I walked out and just kept walking. The mall was huge, humongous. It was in the middle of the desert, sort of speaking, looking like everyday life at this place. I pictured it like some sort of a city inside. There were all these directions and signs and yet I felt lost. All the people were moving, going somewhere. I kept walking… I took a look outside through one of the large windows. Something was going on. It looked hot outside. The air looked like it was burning. It was becoming dark-red along with a strong wind. It was a sand storm. It looked like it was getting tense. It was the first time for me to see such a thing. It was like I was on a different planet. Pressure was hitting the windows, making an odd sound. I looked at that getting bad. Then something hit the window, making a crack on it. No one noticed it. Nothing could be seen outside but fog of sand. The crack became another crack and the window broke. People started screaming while the storm was getting inside. It looked surreal. People were screaming and running while the storm was getting stronger. They started falling off the floors, from stairs. It looked apocalyptic. Like the end of the world. I couldn't see anything anymore. Not even in front of myself. Someone ran into me, pushed me on the floor. I couldn't breathe from the smoke and sand going into my eyes, nose, lungs. I felt pain, powerless to do anything. I kept struggling but was getting overpowered by this. I felt myself drifting slowly to the point I kind of didn't feel anything anymore.

Chapter 5

I woke up, lifted my eyelids. I was lying in bed. It felt soft and smelled good. I was just lying and breathing for a few moments. Then I slowly got up, sat on it. Door was opened. I took a look outside at what looked like a fine day. I stood up, walked out, and took a look around. I looked at the sky. Sun shined brightly. Sky looked clear. So much so that it seemed like I could've seen my own reflection on it if I'd look at it long enough. Then I actually felt myself being present in the woods. No one was around. It was peaceful and quiet. So I sat on the porch. My mind was at total ease. So I have caught myself meditating, feeling the woods sent. Breathing in and out, I felt an odd energy inside and out, but kind of restlessness at the same time. I felt my spirit in some sort of discomfort. Then I thought about that dream I had. Odd thing was that dream led me to this place. I guess I had to figure out how things go from here.

I opened my eyes, and the sun ray warmed my face. I noticed some birds flying. I looked at them imagining if I was a bird for some reason. If I could fly, being totally free. Birds looked light in the sky. Then I thought about those people who shoot at them. That kind of bummed me out. I kind of felt time stood still. At some point I got hungry. So I started to look for food. Any food. But no food I've found. Then I realized I had spent the entire day by myself. Totally alone and I remembered there was a river not far from there. So I found a knife in the house and headed there. After a while of walking, I got there. It looked totally beautiful so much so that I felt bad killing anything there. Not just bad but incapable.

But I was so hungry I was losing my strength, getting weakened. River flowed smoothly, looking clear as the sky. I could actually see life inside of it. I had to improvise so I made a spear. Now, I am a totally clumsy person, but hunger came over me so much that was the only thing I could think about. The river wasn't deep but it was hellishly cold. So I was stepping slowly… looking at the fish swimming. I tried to stab through a few times but that wasn't even close. I may be a clumsy person but far away from quitter and my spear was long enough. I felt kind of silly, but very hungry. So I tried a few more times. Oh man, was I bad at this. I was stepping across the rocks trying to be careful. I tried again and again. And then I just wanted to imagine that I ate and my belly was full. I thought that was easier. I took a look at the sun. It was shining brightly and warm and I felt the fight inside. I felt the rise and fall. I was so hungry that I swear I saw Jesus. He looked at me and I thought well hey, he may just help me to walk on this water or something. He has a thing of appearing at the oddest of times. So I tried again and slipped on the rock. I hit my back, I hit my head, and started bleeding… feeling pain in my entire body. This was great. Now I was fighting for my own life. River color was turning red from my blood. I couldn't move. I saw a fish swimming near me in a color of red. She got closer, like she looked at me and slowly swam away. There goes my lunch, I thought looking at her with my barely opened eyes.

Then I felt like I could move but I couldn't. I couldn't do anything but flout. I ended up somewhere in deeper water feeling totally paralyzed. This was ridiculous. I was going deeper and deeper, slowly.

Then I saw some fish coming my way. She came closer looking at me with her funny eyes.

"Breathe," she said.

"What?"

"Breathe…try to breathe."

"But I can't. I'm not like you. I can't even move."

"Imagine you can. Go on."

So I closed my eyes and tried. But it didn't go well. I was surprised I was alive at that point being underwater for that long. I didn't even know how long that was.

Is this how I end, I thought?

I felt totally numb…I tried to breathe from inside. Then I remembered something. I remembered a feeling when I was a kid I used to be afraid of water. Going in the water I was afraid of deep blue. As time went by, I faced that fear. I learned how to swim and became a good swimmer, I would say. But one time when I was a kid, I was in a small pool with some other kids. I saw some girl floating on her back. That looked interesting to me so I thought I could do it too. But from the moment I tried, I started going down. I started drowning. Water was going into my nose, ears faster I could realize what was going on. I couldn't breathe, my heart was pounding. And I remember the feeling I had thinking, oh, so this is what drowning is like? Well…I didn't quite know what was going to happen. The pool was shallow and I was at the very bottom… looking at the bright, blurry sight before me.

But then someone grabbed me, started pulling. But the hand slipped. I felt it again pulling me up, stronger this time. That was my father. I didn't even know how he saw me. I was four years old.

So there I was, at the bottom of this river, having some sort of close call again, powerless to do anything really.

But then I saw Jesus again, taking my hand, pulling me up. I looked at him. It looked more like his shadow as I was looking up at the sun shining its light through.

Next thing I knew I was on shore somewhere, vomiting, coughing, puking water out… And then I passed out.

*

I woke up in bed, opening my eyes slowly. I had a terrible headache. I couldn't even see where I was. Then someone came. It was a woman. She had something in her hands. She dipped in something that sounded like water and came closer. She sat next to me, smiled at me and started wiping my face gently.

She had long, black hair and was unbelievably pretty. I looked at her thinking is this real or am I hallucinating? Or is it just another God's trick?

"Who are you?" I said.

She kept doing what she was doing, looking at me tenderly.

"Am I dead?"

She put her finger on her lips showing me to be quiet. Then she walked away. I felt so weak I couldn't even think. So I just closed my eyes in pain. I felt like I was struggling with life itself inside. I felt strangely present. I felt myself out there, somewhere, among stars. I felt like I was a wind blowing around among tree tops. I always imagined what it would be like being among stars. I felt it like some sort of magical effect of something that kept me sane. Well, in a way. But it's a fight 'cause nothing comes easy. Not a thing. I knew that well. I have tried to think otherwise. I have failed. So I was in this…odd dream, yet again, far from telling what is what. They say it's good to have dreams. I would say they are right. Mine led me through my entire life like I dreamt it all. And you wake up and some mare goes on. And you lose yourself in it. You get tricked by a feeling that it gets easier.

Few days passed in silence. Or so I think. It was hard for me to tell time in that condition. I remember a man came and looked at me. Or was it a dream?

Anyway, after a while I was able to sit, stand, and walk slowly. My body was weak and it shook.

I didn't really know how badly injured I was but I felt my body was broken.

Well, I was alive.

Man came. He looked at me.

"Good to see you on your feet," he said. "How are you feeling?"

"Kind of silly."

"Does it hurt?"

"I feel new. Can't you tell?"

Man smiled mildly.

"Good to hear you haven't lost a sense of humor."

"Me? Humor and me, we go hand and hand together."

"You must be hungry."

"That I am."

"Come," he said.

We sat and had some soup. We ate for a few moments in silence.

"Well…I guess I was better at catching fish last time."

Man looked at me with a mild smile outlining his face.

"I saw Jesus," I said. "He pulled me out of the water."

"That was me," the man said.

"You? How did you…"

"I saw you and pulled you out."

"You just happen to be there?"

"I'm always around."

"Always around… What does that mean?"

"That means… thinking about me is like thinking about yourself."

"Another riddle."

"Well, it's your mind. We have common reasoning. That is a unique part of who you are. You live your life like so many people. It's powerful and odd. You lose yourself in becoming whoever you want to be. That expands your mind limitlessly. But pain goes with it too. You get to have access to it and that excites you most. If you don't do it… you feel like you don't do anything at all. It's a skill. What can really tell you who you are? You know what I'm talking about?"

I looked at him.

"Writing is peculiar turf. So I ask you… what can you really live without?"

I looked at him. I took a moment. I had nothing. I felt like a blank page. I felt trapped whatever I said. So I said nothing.

Man looked at me smiling, shaking his head. "Is it coming?"

"I came to this world with nothing," I said.

"That is simply not true. You have your family, someone who gave you life, took care of you, gave you home, loved you."

"That's not what I meant."

"Let's hear it."

"Why would I have to choose?"

"Because you have a choice."

"Choice for something I live without?"

"Being complete comes from having nothing. Challenge comes when you start wishing things."

"So what are you saying?"

"I am saying you have a choice, like choosing to come here no matter what you find. Like choosing something at the cost of failure. Like everything that has happened to you so far."

I took some soup.

"What do you think about Gabby?"

"Who?"

"A woman who took care of you."

I needed a moment. "She is nice."

"Nice?"

"She's the most beautiful woman I've ever seen."

"Well… she may just be your salvation."

"Who is she?"

"She doesn't talk much. I was fishing one day and she was swimming. She took very good care of you."

"I thought I was hallucinating."

"Yes, she is very pretty."

"So what's the story?"

"I don't know… but there's the feeling. The right feeling."

Chapter 6

Later that night, we sat around the burning fire after Gabby made us dinner. We had some herbal tea Gabby made as well.

I had some of it looking at the cracking fire while Man was playing guitar. I looked at his hands going over strings. He was playing some slow, smooth sound. It sounded like life. Like something alive. I felt myself being alive listening to that looking at Gabby. It was strange and beautiful.

"Where did you get the guitar?"

"Gary made it," Man said, still playing.

"Where is Gary?"

"Off somewhere. He works a lot. He loses himself in his work. He comes and goes. I wanted you to meet him 'cause I figured it could be… pointing out enough of what he has told you."

"What do you make of it?"

"What do you do? That's the question."

I looked at him.

"Choices, free will. You always believed in that. So this is a place of ways ahead," Man said, still playing. What do you think those ways are?"

"Are you asking me, knowing the answer?"

"What if I do? Would you still act the same?"

"I walked through the dark before."

"I know. But the answer wouldn't necessarily be the same one."

I looked at him playing.

"How long have you been playing?"

"I don't. This is pure improvisation. Like everything in life. Or so I believe. Creation is an amazing thing."

I had some tea.

"I had a dream before the accident."

"A dream?" Man said.

"Of what happened to me… Funny thing, music is the only thing that hasn't been corrupted or broken of all things, dream or reality," I said looking at Man playing.

"That definitely means something,"he said. "So what happened? How did it get broken, like you say?"

"I guess I thought there's more to it. Not just the usual bullshit. I still do."

"That is because you have it in you. That IT. One thing is talking about it and quite another, acting on it. You, my friend, have both. You should be aware of that. You always thought outside of the box, thought big, dreamt big… You have a strong energy and will. But you haven't had the chance to use it yet. I mean really use it."

He played a few more motes, started playing faster.

I looked at him playing and looked at Gabby inside the house, making dinner. She looked amazing, gentle and totally sexy.

I had an odd feeling about sexuality and attraction. Quite honestly, for a long time I was getting a hard on simply towards women I wanted to bang. So the attraction was purely sexual. Was this different? What was this? Who was this lady?

There was definitely something about her. I had this… feeling this woman could change my life. Like a Man said. You really never know who you can meet. Life is funny that way.

Well, I almost died. And now not only was I alive but was looking at a woman I felt something towards. I was laughing inside, I was crying. I was screaming.

I got on my knees. This was the very life I lived. I felt like I was shaping inside. I felt like I was on some kind of drug. Maybe I was. My spirit was alive. It was on fire. I felt it strongly. I felt it raging. And then, I just felt lost in it.

I got up, walked to the house. I came to the door looking at her as she was making something in the kitchen. She was in some shorts and a tight T-shirt. She looked tanned. Like an asian. Like a very sexy malaysian.

"Can I have some more of this tea?" I said.

She turned and looked at me.

"Please?" I said.

She smiled, made a few moves, and took some old looking cattle.

I got close to her, put my cup on the surface she worked on.

She was slowly pouring while I was getting closer to her. I smelled her hair without her noticing. She smelled like wood. I was aroused. So much so my legs were shaking. I was breathing heavily.

I snuggled with her. I touched her neck with my lips over her hair. She was warm, soft and tender. She was strong and smelled good.

I started going over her belly with my hand. I was going over it slowly. I kissed her neck going over her skin with my tongue.

She pulled her head back, breathing deeply. I reached her lips, put my tongue in. She tasted like a fairy. She tasted like honey. I licked her lips, sucking them. She went between my legs with her hands. I pulled her shirt off going over her breasts. They were warm and soft and big. Her nipples made me even harder while our tongues were crossing. It was harder and wetter than ever. And so was she. My fingers were diving as she was breathing, making a light sound. We were all over each other, all hot and sweaty. I felt myself in her hands. She rubbed it, jerked it. I just slid in. I felt warmth. I felt some sort of hope. This wasn't just an act, this was a wonder. Oh my God. I felt free. I felt happy and free. I was drugged by this. I was struck by lightning. I felt like a rock. I felt life inside of me going wild. Yes… This was it.

Well, let me tell you… If anybody asks you, are you afraid of death? Tell then to fuck off. Fuck that. Fuck dying. I will fucking die with the fucking smile on my face. With this amazing hard on all wet and hard, singing. I would light a cigarette but I don't smoke. But this life I feel inside does. Fuck you death, fuck you pain. This is all it's real. You want to die? Do it hard. Don't be a fucking pussy.

I was hitting hers while I held her ass tight. Her sweet, sexy ass was shaking while I was hitting. Oh my God.

There come soldiers, blood thirsty for fight. Battle dressed in white. They were running like I was hitting fast in her sweet, sexy ass.

That is when I came. I went out on a light. I looked at it shining bright. This was nowhere… yet there was light. Light meant life shined bright. Shine on life. Once you don't, we'll be gone.

So I looked at the light that looked back at me when I heard the voice…

"You want to play something?" Man said.

I held a cup being strangely conscious of whether I lost my mind.

I took a look at Gabby inside the house being busy with something.

"You want to try?"

"I don't… play."

"You all right?"

"Yeah… I'm fine…" I said unsurely.

Good thing he couldn't read my mind.

"Try it," he said. "See where it takes you."

I went with my hand over my face like I was possessed or something.

Man passed the guitar and I measured in my lap. I took a deep, long breath in and out.

"Whatever you do, free your mind."

I was listening to the woods for a moment. I looked at the fire. Then I looked at Gabby.

This was quite a state of mind.

I started playing. Well I started something. It sounded like something. I dare to say. I didn't know what I was doing except for looking at my hands , going over strings, making sounds. So I just played… looking at the woods. It looked like a deep, darkish place yet amazing, like you could get lost easily. I felt quite lost. So lost that I wasn't sure of finding my way back. Whatever back that is or may be.

Gabby called for dinner.

We came in. It all looked like dames hands work of art. Everything was at its place. We even had music.

We had dinner in silence while music was playing.

"Oh my God…" I said after finishing, holding my belly. "I will never leave this place. Thank you for a wonderful dinner lady."

She smiled. Her cheeks were pinkish as well as her lips.

Then a song started playing. I wished for nothing but dancing.

So I got up, took her hand and we started dancing.

Music is a cure for the soul… and more.

Dancing along I felt her like the light I saw. And yet I was kind of in the dark of the great ahead, unknown though. But it was ok. The feeling was right, like the Man had said.

I didn't know who they were. They seemed to know more about me. Yet, there we were, kind of happy in this story of mine with not a soul for miles around.

Music echoed in the woods in the dark, picturing the house and us dancing inside.

We danced long into the night. Music played and candle light shined bright.

Chapter 7

When I woke up the next morning, the sun shined directly at me. I felt it so close to it I could smell it. I shield my eyes with my hand. I smelled something... It was wood and candle smoke. I took a deep breath, meditating for a moment.

I got up, went out. The woods looked unreal. Sun shined bright through it. It looked so alive and colorful. I felt I was awakened in another world. River flowed smoothly with a humming sound. It was quite a scene. Like a postcard. Funny thing... I haven't seen any animals since I came here aside from birds and fishes in the river. Maybe I imagined them too... as far as I could tell at this point.

I saw a Man and Gabby, doing something by the river.

"Good morning," Man said, stepping towards me.

"It looks amazing."

"It does, doesn't it?"

"Cold, though."

"Well, winter is coming. Would you like some coffee?"

"Absolutely."

Man went in. I stayed on the porch, looking around. I looked at Gabby. Man brought us two cups filled with black liquid.

"Thank you."

"Here... I brought you a blanket," he said.

"Thanks."

I sat on the chair and put it around me. I had some coffee, listening to silence and peace.

"So you mentioned you had a dream," Man said.

"It was a dream of what happened."

"What was that?"

"The world I don't… know how to believe in. The world I don't trust."

"Tell me more."

"However I try to talk about it… it's gonna sound weird."

Man looked at me.

"I remember being a kid. A young boy, innocent, funny looking. Most of the time I felt like I was sort of dreaming. Oddly though, I didn't care much for reality. I felt something inside that led me, blindly sometimes. When you care for something you go for it, whatever it takes. Well… that's me at least. I felt that changing over time. I didn't like what I felt. I wasn't sure who I was, what to do. I was lost. I felt lost. But sometimes being lost can be a powerful guide. So I just became flat lined. I'm not a particularly religious person but I've realized, without compassion you are as good as dead. With no journey, it's like you haven't really lived. With no expression or action, you are just another brick in the wall. So I guess… I've lost it all. All the senses. I couldn't recognize them anymore. I couldn't feel them anymore. I thought of what to do to get them back. Well, that's when you showed up."

I had some coffee.

"Moving on is part of who you are too. And now, there's her right there."

"So, what… She just appeared?" I said looking at her.

"Don't think about that much. She is here. That's what matters. Why don't you go talk to her?"

I finished my coffee, got up and started walking towards her.

"Knock, knock on heaven's door,"I said, smiling, getting close.

She smiled, washing some clothes.

"How's it going?"

"Good," she said." And you?"

"Ok, Thanks. I want to thank you for taking care of me. You saved my life."

"I wouldn't say that,"she said.

"Trust me, you did."

She kept doing what she was doing.

"So how long have you been here?"

"A while, and you?"

"Around the same. Quite a place, ha?"

"Yes."

"I had a very nice time last night," I said. "You know your way with food and dancing."

She smiled."That was all you."

"No, no…" we both smiled. "You surely have some moves. Maybe we could do it again sometime."

"Yeah, sure. I am glad you had a nice time."

"Nice it was."

"So Gabby, right?"

"Yes."

"Well, I'm Mark."

She smiled. "I know."

"Right. Do you need any help?"

"No, I'm good. Thanks."

"You know… it's strange talking to you at this very moment since I almost died. Twice that is. Some would call it lucky. I call it beating the odds. So when that becomes your life, you take a chance especially when you have nothing to lose. And now there's you. You mean something. Actually, you mean everything. Man said you are my salvation. And yet, I don't know much about you. But there's this feeling… I'm sorry… Do I bore you?"

"No. I haven't had a conversation this long for some time."

I couldn't tell if she was sarcastic or romantic. Or what she was.

"Where are you from?" I said.

"I will tell you some other time. Man knows," she said smiling.

"He does?"

I looked at him sitting on the porch.

"Well, I guess I'll leave you to it then. We'll do something later. I want to know more about your music taste, dancing and food."

I smiled and so did she.

So we kind of became a man and a woman. We were spending time together. I sat around and simply looked at her while she did stuff. There was a certain style to it. I didn't want to ask too many questions.

Actually, I didn't ask anything at all. She definitely looked like a woman with some sort of secret. Everybody has secrets. Just so it happens it gets on the surface. It's like being long under water. You simply have to get on top. Or you drown.

Well, in every man's life there should be a woman and vice versa. That's just natural law. We are simple creatures. But we have a tendency to make things complicated. And so that becomes our life. And we suffer. It is a big trick we get fooled by a tale of pursuit.

So I was thinking. Was I tricked by this? Was I tricked by the presence of this woman? I looked at her while music was playing while she was making food, while she was dancing. Could this be that simple? Could it be what it seems to be?

So I did what the Man had said. I just didn't think about it. I went with it instead.

We didn't speak much. We just did stuff together. We were dancing, walking, and making food together. It felt like pure improvisation, like playing music. Like life itself.

One day, she took me to some place. We walked through the woods and came to some shore. God knows how she knew about it. It was a whole day away.

"This is how the world looks to me," she said looking at it.

It was quite a sight. The rocks and the water and sun were looking magical on the horizon.

"It looks like quite a world," I said.

She came closer to me and looked at me. Then she kissed me. It was a long, sweet kiss. I felt complete and free. I didn't want to think about anything else, absolutely.

I hugged her deep and tight, feeling her entire body. I felt both of our hearts beating.

"This is where I came when I first got here," she said.

"From where?"

She looked at me.

"Far away land…"

"Ok."

"It looks different every time. That's kind of the beauty of it."

"It's getting dark."

"You scared?"

I shook my head.

"Look at it…" she said.

It did look magical. Like the existence of another world. Like some sort of parallel universe.

"Sometimes I think we are made of this," she said looking at the sight.

"It's quite an existence. Like it was when I first saw you. After… well, you know. I thought I was hallucinating.".

She mildly smiled.

"You are the most beautiful sight I've ever seen."

I looked at her and she looked at me. I took her hand and we watched the world's natural course while stars were appearing. We stood there, two people in the dark.

I looked at this place and felt I could strangely disappear inside. I felt all these different versions of myself. Like a spirit that wanders around. I was there and everywhere at the same time. Yet I felt a threat of some kind. Or was it just my mind?

Don't be afraid, I heard a voice inside. Don't be afraid. Just be present, voice said. However you see it fits. The rest of the world doesn't exist. You have got the strength, will and power of every minute and every hour. It is really up to you what your world is like inside and out. It is a fight and you have to fight like you always have to tell what's real or not. That is who you are. So don't be afraid. Just play your part. All the rest will work out.

I kept looking at the sight and then I noticed something. It looked like some kind of light on water. The light was getting bigger, closer. Then I heard something. Like tap on water.

"Anyone there?" the voice said.

Light shined on me.

"Mark?"

"Yeah…"

"It's Gary. Are you all right?"

"Yeah… I guess."

"Do you need a lift?"

I looked at Gabby. She looked at me. I didn't even think about a way back.

"Sure Gary. That'll be nice of you."

"Jump in," he said.

We got in and he started paddling.

"You are pretty far away. How did you end up here?"

"We were just walking…" I said while Gabby looked the other way.

"Where did you come from?"

"Oh I do this often…" Gary said. „Day or night, it doesn't matter. It's kind of a sport to me."

"You have a spare paddle?" I said. "I could dip in too."

"Sure. Go ahead."

I took the other one and we paddled.

"So what do you think of the place?" Gary said.

"I'm not sure if I can put in one word."

"Hmmm…" Gary mumbled. "Well, I've seen things here."

I looked at him.

"What things?"

"All sorts. I move in the dark a lot. I move fast. It's nice and romantic. But it knows to be… different too."

"Yeah, I know. I almost died."

"Yeah I heard. You are lucky."

"Yeah… lucky," I said after a moment, looking at Gabby.

We paddled in silence looking around. Gary was smoking.

Night sky was clear with so many stars I couldn't count and the moon was shining bright.

I looked at that, thinking about the space above… and man's words that everything is connected. We are able to create and do so much and yet, we contradict ourselves. We get lost in our own sense of reasoning for our own existential urges to pleasure ourselves. I guess that makes us humans. The world we live in is really beyond our understanding and control. We are destroying it more than we know and we don't realize it. When, in fact, the world is beautiful. And our lives are precious while we take it for granted.

When we came back it was all in black and dark all around. The only light was coming from the moon and clear sky.

We went into the house and Gabby lit a candle. I lied on the bed breathing deeply. I closed my eyes, being still. Then I opened them and looked at the dark.

"Have you seen any animal since you've been here?"

"Animal? No, why?"

"No reason. Just thinking I'd see one for all this time being here."

"I've heard voices."

"Voices? What kind of voices?"

"I don't know. Just voices."

She came to bed and lied next to me. I looked at her. She had her eyes closed. I heard her breathing like she was drifting into deep sleep. I wished I could sleep. Instead I listened to silence and the river nearby. I felt strangely conscious about being on that bed, at that place. My spirit was restless. I saw myself dancing around while music was playing. Like nothing mattered. Like I didn't care if there's tomorrow I looked at myself dancing as if that was the only thing I knew. That made me smile. I danced and danced looking silly. Like a ghost on candle light. Music kept playing so I kept dancing till deep in the night. So much so, that I can't tell was I dreaming or did I go nuts?

But dare I say I was happy. Or again, was I just silly or just far, far away? But it was all right. I didn't know where I was heading nor how. But I felt the moment now. And that was the thing of dream and reality I could say for sure.

Chapter 8

When I opened my eyes I heard something from outside. It was some music playing. I was just lying for a few moments. Then I looked at Gabby. She was still sleeping.

I got up, walked out. Sun shined brightly. It was a fine day.

I saw someone sitting, back resting on a tree. It was a Man playing guitar not far away from his boat.

I walked to him. He looked at me while I walked, tapping his foot on the ground in the spirit of the rhythm he was playing.

"Did I wake you?" he said.

"No. I see you are getting deep into this."

"This thing grows on me. Music is magic."

"That it is."

"Like someone once said... It's like having sex without touching."

We both smiled.

"Speaking of it..." he looked at me.

"How's it going?"

"Ok, I guess..."

He kept playing... looking around like measuring the words.

"So you are in good hands there?"

"I'm not sure what that is. But I'm going with it."

I looked at him. "You know more than you say. About her, I mean."

"Why do you say that?"

"She mentioned something. Maybe she was kidding."

"I've told you who she is and could be. The rest is totally up to you."

I sat down while he still played.

"Maybe I should start a bend." I looked at him.

He burst into laughter "Maybe not."

"I think you could."

"So do you think about going back?"

"Back?"

"Yeah."

"I don't... know how to go back. To what?"

"Well, eventually you will. And now, there's her."

I looked at the river.

"You are a part of it whether you like it or not. There is no easy way out. No matter where you are. You know that. There will always be struggles. That's the nature of it all. But the struggle holds a reward. You know what I'm talking about? Nothing is what it seems. Not even this place. And you can always come back, I guess. It wouldn't be the same though. You don't go through something twice the same way. This is happening now. Right now."

I was angry just listening to his words. But he was right. It was almost as if I forgot why I came here at all. I felt it boiling inside. I felt the fight. That fight was nothing but the feeling. Feelings can trick you and lead you to the abyss. This emotion was raw and I was deep in... feeling kind of the same way when I was drowning. I felt like jumping into that river and letting it take me. I felt like I was possessed. Or was it a test? I felt anger growing inside. Like a powerful force of evil. I felt a taste of it. It was tightening me inside, crushing me like I was crumbling stone.

Being that way, I could see this whole place burned to the ground. But I didn't want to be that way. I didn't want to be like the world is. Like the way it became. I didn't want to be led by other forces but my choices. I didn't want to be another sheep in a herd. I refuse to be. And all of you who read this, you must never be. Dare to live your life the way you want to live whatever that may be. Don't wait for others to point you in directions. Choose your own. You can do it. If I can, you can. We have one thing in common. We are humans.

"Are you ok?" Man looked at me. "You seem a bit off."

"I'm fine."

"Where did you go just now?"

I smiled "I'm always somewhere inside."

"Does it work?"

"It's kind of like meditating."

"Yes. It's all about finding the way."

Later that day we had lunch. We had it in silence. After that, Man left.

Gabby and I went for a walk. She knew the path down the river. We didn't speak much. We held each other's hands. We hugged one another.

We came back and Gabby made us dinner. I watched her doing it. I watched her moving around. We ate in silence.

She went out to wash some clothes in the river. I just sat at the table, bent on my elbow… looking outside. I looked at the light as the sun was leaving while setting. It looked so simple and beautiful. It had a peculiar and careful effect. Or was it my imagination? I have a tendency to lose myself in this. Or was it my own mind I couldn't find?

I looked at that in peace and quiet when she came in.

She lit some candles, came closer to me. She pulled out her hand, watching me smile. I pulled out mine and we went to bed.

We looked at each other. I looked at her eyes. She looked at mine. Then, I couldn't help myself any more. I went for it and kissed her. Long, sweet and slow with her tongue against mine.

They say kissing has an effect of happiness. Similarly, I like eating chocolate. Well, let's say they are right. I can't quite remember if I was ever happier having my tongue in her mouth feeling her entire body. She took me in her hands, started playing. If this wasn't happiness then I don't know what is.

We kept kissing while I was going over her breasts. Her big, soft, juicy breasts. I was rock hard. She was hellishly wet. This foreplay was a path to heaven.

She took me in her mouth and started licking. I grabbed her ass, pulled my tongue in. I came in her mouth. She kept going. I felt I was putting my tongue inside a volcano. A bit closer to heaven. Then she came. I kept going.

She sat on me.

"I want to see you," she said.

She started swinging, breathing deeply. I grabbed her ass, her breasts. My hands were all over her. She jumped like every next move was her last one. She jumped so hard I thought she was going to break it. And yet again she came, pulling her head back.

We rolled. I took her from behind and started hitting. Her ass was warm and sweaty. Like two hand grenades. I was hitting so fast I thought my heart was going to explode. Her ass shook. She didn't make a sound. I kept hitting. I rolled her over putting her knees around my neck. Again, I was in. This was it. I was close. Here it goes... She looked melted like cheese. So was I. She closed her eyes, bending her head back. I started shooting bullets inside... until I was totally dry out of strength, out of breath, out of life. I just dropped on the bed breathing fast. That was all I can remember before I simply fell asleep.

Chapter 9

It was early morning when I opened my eyes. She was still sleeping. I felt like running so I went for a run. I ran down the river path. I felt charged. Like the shining sun I felt alive. I kept running and running... and then I walked, catching a breath.

Then I heard a sound. Some kind of noise that sounded distant. But then it sounded closer and closer. I ran off the path without noticing. So now I didn't know where I was. I looked around but all I saw was more woods. Every direction looked the same.

I was lost in the woods before. But it was quite a small one and I wasn't alone.

I looked in all directions and I took one. I walked and walked... It's kind of odd when you hear yourself like the only one in the woods.

After a while of walking I had no idea where I was. Then I saw something. It was a cliff. How in hell did I end up here?

I came closer. It was a small cliff with a view on the rest of the woods. I looked at it when I heard something from behind. I turned but no one was there. I kept looking... kept hearing the sound. I thought of how to find the way back, when I saw him.

He looked like a wolf as far as I could tell. I've never seen one in person. Now I have. He looked dangerous and angry. Hungry so much so the foam was drooling out of his jaw.

This was great. I had nowhere to go and nothing to defend myself with and he looked in his way of killing me and eating me.

He moved closer, slowly. I was totally powerless and cornered against him on a little cliff of a few steps. His jaw looked monstrous. His eyes looked blood thirsty.

"Who made you this way buddy? Is it me? Or you simply see me as food?"

I looked at him and he looked at me. I wanted him to recognize goodness in my eyes but it didn't work. I simply didn't know what to do as he was getting closer.

I imagined closing my eyes and trying to feel nothing as he jumped on me.

I could try to fight him back but I didn't stand the chance like this. Ah, fuck it. I wished I had that knife back from fish hunting day. That way he wouldn't stand a chance. I was shitty out of luck.

Then I remembered something. One day I walked the street I lived in. I was going to a neighbor's house. I can't remember why. That neighbor had two dogs barking at everybody right at the gates. They were such annoying little creatures. Everybody hated them.

That day I went there and called my neighbor from outside. Dogs were at the gates, barking like insane. No one answered. I tried a few more times, nothing. That's when I went in. I don't know why I did it. I just went in. I wasn't thinking. I just did it. Dogs barking jaws were right next to my leg so close I could feel their breath. Me going in made them even more mad. Seeing that I realized what I did. But there was no going back.

So by some chance they didn't bite me. I don't know how or why neither my neighbor when she finally opened the door and chased them away.

Now, I was in front of this creature… trying to figure out what would be a move.

He was ready to jump. I saw some rock a few steps back. I went for it while he was a couple steps away. I grabbed it but then I tripped. I know. I am the clumsiest person you will ever meet. What can I tell you…

And not just that, the ground under my feet crumbled at the very edge. So now I was falling down the abyss… rolling. Everything was spinning… until I hit some tree.

I must have fallen unconscious or something. When I opened my eyes it was dark. I felt pain and dust in my mouth. I checked myself if anything was broken. Luckily it wasn't.

I slowly got up, looked around. I saw nothing but woods and darkness. I looked up… the way I fell from. It looked high. I started laughing. Well, I was alive.

I took some direction. I moved on.

I was thinking well, I know about three people living here. What if somebody else is out here? That was me comforting myself going through dark woods.

I tried to orient myself. I listened to sounds. I looked at the sky above. I tried to find the river. I felt like the woods swallowed me into her belly.

So I just kept walking… hoping to run on someone or something.

But it didn't happen.

After walking for a long time, I sat next to some tree. They surely noticed me not being there so I figured it was just a matter of time till they found me. Again, I was comforting myself.

I sat there waiting… until I saw the light of dawn. I saw a fog widening the woods like some kind of ghost in silence. It looked kind of creepy yet amazing. It was getting cold and I was getting hungry. I imagined that wolf on a stick. Sorry wolfy. I felt my body eating itself. I felt I was losing weight. I was losing strength.

But then I found some mushrooms. I couldn't tell if they were poisonous or not. I was hungry so I said to hell with it and stuffed my mouth with them.

I took some with me as much as I could carry. I memorized where I found them. Well, I thought I did.

I thought about what to do. I tried to recall some places but they were dead ends. What if I came across another animal? A bear or something… That's even worse than a wolf. I had no weapon, no tools, nothing I could defend myself with, nothing to point me anywhere. All I had was mushrooms.

I moved on…and on. Then rain started falling. But it wasn't like ordinary rain. It was falling fiercely like angry. I have never seen rain falling like that. So I looked for cover. Rain was falling so hard I could hardly see in front of myself.

I amazingly found something that looked like some kind of a cave. I went into the dark. Rain looked like a curtain of fog from inside.

I was soaked. Where in hell was I?

It wasn't cold inside. Not that I could feel from where I was. I couldn't see anything inside just a few steps away from me.

So I sat down, bent on a wall. The wall was warm. So I just sat there... looking at the angry rain falling.

I tried to think about something nice and warm. But nothing of the sort had an effect. Man was right. Sometimes there is no escape. Just covers, as it appears. I liked the smell though. I couldn't tell what that was, rain, rocks and ground?

I took some rocks I'd found and, to my surprise, I made a fire. Now, I could see deeper into the cave. I couldn't believe I made that fire. It was small but just enough to warm me up. And dry my clothes. And if you notice, I even had music.

Rain was falling, making a sound. Fire was cracking, making it as well.

I closed my eyes and imagined more of it. Music was saving my life and it was doing it again. I took some mushrooms, just chewed them. Oh man did they taste like chocolate. Like heaven if there is one.

Funny thing... I didn't like them when I was a kid. I didn't trust the taste. But then my life became all about food and so taste changed. Now they are all I could eat.

I kept chewing them, getting sleepy. I felt myself drifting slowly.

"You can't deny the irony..." I heard the voice say.

I opened my eyes and saw a face that looked like mine in a dark corner. It looked like the face of a clown. I looked at it.

"You came here looking for... answers. And this place keeps trying to kill you," face had said.

I looked at the face and then I looked at the mushroom I held in my hand.

"I liked that peach though. I could hit that peach for hours. Best I've ever had."

"Why do you look like a clown?" I said.

"'Cause you feel like one."

I looked at the face and turned my head looking at emptiness.

"So what do you think it's gonna happen here?" face said. „I mean really... You are out here totally alone, all by yourself. They are probably looking for you right now but you don't know where you are. Nor where you need to go," face shook its head pointlessly. "More woods you cross, the more you will be lost."

I took a deep breath in and out. I closed my eyes.

Face smiled clownishly. „Go ahead, ignore. See where that gets you. This place is not what you think it is, nor what you want it to be. Or haven't you figured that out? Can you say for sure if everything really happened the way it did at this point? Is it real or simply fake? Your mind plays tricks on you."

"Shut up."

"Shutting me up is not gonna make it any less true. You were always like that. Always better in imagining, manufacturing... then actually living. Imagine you die in this cave which is likely. No soul would miss you. That is sad. Even for a clown. Your chances are slim pal. Sorry. And your time is running out."

Face clownishly laughed. And then it was gone. Fire was gone too. Now there was dark and silence.

It was night time and I could amazingly see the sky from there. It was all clear and pretty. And I thought well, maybe there's really a God out there somewhere. I tried to think like one. What does God think? Does he think at all? Or simply acts? Does he have someone to do it for him? Maybe he has slaves. Or someone you could call it that.

I wish to get face to face with him. They say there is one in every living person. Is that how the world evolves? By putting a seed into the mind of every living thing?

Well, everybody believes in something in their own way even the ones who lose their faith. The world of today is confusing to say the least. Our faith gets shaken. Is that God's act too? Or something went extremely wrong?

I picture God as a guilty one, sitting in the interrogation room, answering for all he does. He's explaining everything so we can finally understand who he is, what he is, and what it all means.

Well, I wonder what his message would be. What would he say?

One thing is for sure. He would have a lot to answer for. Who or whatever he is.

That's when I closed my eyes, but before I knew it I saw a morning light.

I thought about what I should do. Should I leave or should I stay?

I got up, went for food and to think about it some more.

So I stayed. But soon I ran out of food. It's been days and nights... or was it weeks since I had seen a living being, since I looked at myself in a mirror.

It got colder in a cave more than I could bear and yet, anyway, I stayed.

My beard had grown as well as my hair. I had lost weight. I looked like a real caveman. Like a ghost, a spook, a child story before bedtime. My body was eating itself the same as my brain as if I could feel ants wiggling on it, eating it alive.

Then snow started falling. I looked at it thinking, am I seeing this or is it real? I couldn't tell any more. I needed to move on. I needed to get out of there or I was going to die. Like the clown's face said.

So I did. I moved on. I was fighting my way through the woods while snow was falling. It looked kind of romantic I have to say. So quiet, mysterious and deadly in a way.

I was skinny and weak but I kept going. As long as I kept going, that kept me alive. Although it crossed my mind to just lie down and die. Fuck you death. I'm still here. Even if the end may be near. I'm still here. I imagined myself being strong for this. That was the only thing keeping me alive.

I'd found some food. Don't ask me what. It was edible. Then I heard something. I heard a sound getting louder and closer. I saw something looking like a helicopter flying my way. I watched him flying over, flying away...

I looked at the direction it came from and in that moment I felt saved.

So I kept going. A lot of woods were ahead... but I just didn't care.

Snow was still falling and now it was all white. My lungs got cold. I walked the entire day. And then I had to stop. I'd found some big trees. I sat under one. I took some snow, melted it in my hand and drank it.

Night sky was clear again. I saw some light show on it. It looked like a polar light. It was pretty sensational. I missed Gabby. I missed the man too. Well, I could still run into them or Gary. I wondered how likely that is. Light show was gone in the sky. I ate some more snow. There was no way for me to stay there. If I did, I'd die. So I got up and moved on.

I didn't know what was ahead of me. I took a direction based on a sign I saw for which I had to convince myself that I actually saw it.

I wandered the woods, walking the entire night. I was hungry, I was cold. I thought my head was going to explode. Good thing I could eat snow even if it came from a God's but.

And then the storm started. Like out of the blue. Strong wind started blowing... carrying snow all around like God was mad or something. There were no covers, no shelters, just a lot of trees. It was me against it.

I tried to hide behind them. Wind was so strong it was breaking them.

I stepped somewhere and fell through. I felt a strong hit slamming on the ground. I wasn't moving. I just stayed like that. I couldn't do anything. I couldn't feel anything. All I could do was breathe. At that moment I thought I died.

Chapter 10

And then I saw the light. I opened my eyes and saw it coming from above. It was a long beam of sunlight shining bright. I didn't know if I was dead or alive. For a few moments I didn't do anything but be still. I looked at the light, I looked around...and then I tried to move slowly.

I stood up on my feet looking around. It looked like some kind of a hole and that sun beam was the only source of light. There was nothing there but dust.

I looked at that and then I looked at the top. It wasn't too high. It didn't seem so. I knew there was no point of yelling, no one would hear me. So I didn't bother. I checked the wall and tried to climb. Not good enough. I kept trying but all I did was sliding. I had to get out of this while there was light. But that light was getting weaker by the minute.

Finally, after a whole day of trying, I somehow managed to get a grip. I was almost there but then a rock came off, my leg slid... I fell and twisted my joint. I started yelling, pushing all the pain out. I think the entire woods heard that.

I just laid there watching my joint getting bigger, all swollen. Good thing was I could move it.

I forced myself to get up, finding my balance, looking up.

Then I felt desperation and anger, madness growing inside. I started pushing the wall with both hands, yelling... I was hitting it, punching it, till I got on my knees. I was shaking and crying. I strengthen myself on my knees. I closed my eyes just breathing deeply and slowly. That calmed me down. I got up, looked at the wall. I took a deep breath looking at the way out. I started climbing slowly and carefully, move by move. I was doing good and then I grabbed onto something. Something I literally pulled out of the wall. It was some root or something I was just hoping it would hold. I kept climbing and pulling slowly and carefully.

So I made my way through. I rolled at the top, laid on the ground, just watching the sky. I started laughing. I laughed as if the sky could hear me. I wondered if anybody ever died from laughing. I felt kind of absurd.

I got up, looked around... It was night time. It was cold. I saw my breath in the air. There was no other way of walking, but limping. A whole night was ahead of me and a whole lot of woods. Well, again, I was alive. I felt it like a blessing and a curse. I felt like I became something else than human. Like revenant or something.

There was a moon shining above in its full glare. I didn't notice it by then. It looked pretty. It shined a light on the sky peacefully.

I kept walking. Well, limping. Imagining it was all good.

I remembered a story about a man surviving in nature's cruel conditions, a true story about a man, an explorer, who got attacked by a bear who almost killed him. He was left to die by his team. He was injured, totally by himself. All he could do was to crawl. Yet he managed to survive. He amazingly fought his way. I was fascinated with his story. I was amazed with his will and strength to survive. He fought until his very last breath.

They made a movie about him. And now the whole world knows about it.

I tried to imagine how he must have felt crossing miles and miles of uncharted land. Pretty much like me, at this point.

Nothing worked. Nothing I could've ease the pain with. Nothing I could do. I didn't even know how I managed to be on my feet in the state I was.

I thought what if I stop for a short while, sit under some tree and close my eyes. But I seriously thought if I fell asleep I may not wake up. Maybe I was paranoid. And then I did make a stop. I held onto some tree just breathing the air in and out.

I took some snow mixed with the ground. I looked at that in my hand... and put it in my mouth. I tried to chew it, tried to swallow it. I felt something squirreling in my mouth. I took some more. There were some red little bugs looking like ants as far as I could see in the dark. So I ate them. I had no idea what that was, nor what it could do to me. I honestly didn't care.

The air started to smell good. I sensed from the trees. That smell always takes me back to the very first time I sensed it at sea.

And then it hit me... What if the sea is somewhere nearby? No. No way. I denied it by asking a question to myself at the same time.

I stood up, looking ahead. I was getting inspired yet fighting with my instinct, the very basic one. To survive, or was it a dead man talking?

I moved on.

After a while, the sky was getting brighter. Dawn was coming. I saw a hill in the distance. I looked at it as I was getting closer. It was something that looked like a hill.

I came to it, took a look for a moment. Then I started to climb. I was making my way to the top. When I finally made it I was taken by the sight. I looked at miles and miles of nothing but woods and mountains.

Light of dawn was making its way on the horizon. Rising sun fought its way through...

When I was a kid I used to think that whenever I saw sunrise or sunset or clear sky with a lot of stars and moon shining bright, a God would make an appearance. Well, he never would, of course. I'd move on with a mind-bug inside, a question. What is really out there? Every single night since I can remember, I look up and look at the sky with the same question.

I looked at the endless sight, then I got on my knees, strengthless, I went over my head with my hands, desperately.

As much as the sight was pretty, breathtaking actually, a thought came through my mind, sharp as a knife. A thought that in fact, I won't make it and this thing was the last thing I'll see? I beat death enough times to take a chance with this oddity.

Sun was rising. I looked at the sight having a feeling I was on fucking Mars or something. They say a person can be rich by how many sun rises and sets he sees for their lifetime.

Was this the last of mine?

I had two choices, to move on or lie down and die. Well I liked the first one better.

I looked at the sunrise, gaining my strength. I got up watching the entire sight. I closed my eyes and hoped for the best.

Day turned into a hot one. I can't remember if I ever saw a bigger sun shining brighter in the sky. I couldn't even look at it.

I kept crossing the unknown land as I had for days and nights, more than I could count. More than I would care to bear in mind. All that land was ahead of me looking all threatening and everything. I stopped to catch a breath. I looked around thinking about where I was.

Then I saw myself laying dead not far away from where I was standing. I looked at that. Fuck you. Fuck that. Get a grip. Don't be a pussy. I felt my body step from fading.

So after…I don't know how long of a walk, I saw it. At first I thought my mind was playing tricks while I was getting closer. It looked unreal to be true. It looked like a dream. I felt I was in one as I was walking, looking at it. I could sense the smell of it.

I made my way through, getting out of the woods, stepping on sand. I made a few more steps looking at the shore.

I was out. I still couldn't believe what I saw.

I stood hypnotized…then turned around slowly looking at the woods behind me.

It looked like a big, cruel monster.

I turned back, watching the shore, making my moves on sand, getting closer.

I stepped into shallow water going over my feet. I bend on my knees. I put my hands in and out. I watched water dripping from them. I watched my wet palms…

I looked around… I saw big rocks, different shapes in close distance. Crystal clear water was spreading infinitely.

I felt I'd discovered some kind of a new world or something.

Sun was setting beautifully in its own fashion… leaving smeared colors on the sky behind.

I took some water in my hands and started drinking. This was beyond the very existence. Beyond hunger, beyond thirst, beyond survival. This was a beauty of its kind. And I was alive to witness it. It was beyond words really. Beyond minds… well beyond mine anyway.

Shore was spreading all the way a sight could reach. I was still trying to wrap my head around this. Sun went down. It was getting dark and cold. I had to move on.

But which way?

All directions looked the same. I'd flip a coin if I had one. I looked for some signs. Any sign. But I saw nothing. So I said fuck it and went with my gut.

I walked on sand looking at waves. I thought about dropping on that sand and just waiting for the morning. But it was too cold. I'd reached this far so I just didn't think about it. Thinking about it could get me killed. Like when I saw myself lying dead in the woods. Although I felt like a ghost at this place, in this dark night I felt like a dead man walking.

At moments it was like I couldn't tell if I was really lying dead there or was I just a spirit that wanders now?

And then, at some point, I saw something that kind of saved my life.

I was walking, getting close to it, trying to see what that was.

I saw a light or something. Something was there. Somebody was there.

As I was approaching I heard a sound of music playing. I saw people, many people. I pinched myself. I felt pain. Ok this was real.

I saw a crowd of people dancing, lying on sand. Some of them were in the water. They were all drinking, having fun.

I started going through the crowd, looking like some kind of crazy person. I looked at all the people in a subtle shock. I looked at half naked girls dancing around me with their eyes closed.

No one noticed me. This felt like a meteor had struck. I watched them all, walking slowly.

"Hey pal…You all right?" someone said. I saw two gays with a beer bottles in their hands, standing near.

I just looked at them like I forgot how to speak.

"You all right?" they said again.

No words. I felt weak. I felt like something was taking a life out of me. I was fading inside. And then I felt nothing. I dropped to my knees and fell on the sand.

Chapter 11

I woke up in a hospital looking at the white ceiling. I could tell by the smell. It was quiet. I was the only one in the room. I was dressed in some hospital clothes under which I had nothing.

I'd noticed the big window on the other side of the room. I tried to move. I got up slowly, took a few steps, and kept walking toward the window.

It was daytime. I came close to it, looking through it. I saw the world like an image. I saw it the way it was. It was no different from the way it was all in smoke and pollution. It looked like a time bomb. It looked like it was going to its end.

I saw sick, poor and hungry people. I saw people on the streets. I saw people killing other people. I saw destruction. I saw danger and confusion. People made it that way. People got used to living in that mess. Some say it's a perfect mess for what's coming. No one believes in the end of the world. It's a big joke.

I looked at that world from that window... thinking what is going to happen. Is it possible for Earth to just explode one day? One fine day, like it never existed? Is there a life anywhere else? I think about it every time I look at the sky.

Maybe it should collapse.... the end of something for the beginning of something else. Maybe that is the way it's going to be. Well, we'll see.

I kept watching all I saw through the window. And then, I saw someone standing on the street, looking at the window I was standing next to. That someone looked familiar. I took a better look and saw the

Man walking. He was just standing there, smiling, looking at me, with his hands in his pockets. He looked secretive as he was from the very moment I met him. At this very moment I still didn't know who he was. I figured to leave things that way. He waved at me. He smiled and waved. I waved back, discreetly.

And then, something started to change. Something was happening, something in the sky. Dark clouds came. And now, everything was dark. Wind started to blow.

I took a look at where the Man was. He was gone. I looked for him but I didn't see him.

There was a storm outside looking angrier and angrier. Wind blew profusely. So much so, it shook the gravity. It looked like the whole hell was breaking loose.

A black bird slammed on the window and scared the life out of me. She was dead leaving the stains of blood behind. I looked at that blood gliding. The window was cracked now. Sky was red. Clouds were dark. It really looked like hell if there was one. Maybe the devil was making an appearance. Maybe this was his work all along.

Whatever it was, it was bad. It looked like Earth was bleeding. Like the sky was burning.

Crack on a window became another crack. I started stepping back slowly. Wind hit it and broke a part of it. Countless pieces of glass ended up on the floor. Wind rolled the bed and smashed on the wall. I fell down trying to guard myself. Wind was making a devilish sound.

Then I thought to myself... if it's possible that all of this was just in my head? A dream within a dream, where I got so lost that I couldn't tell what's real. I couldn't tell if I was dreaming or awake?

Well, how about that?

That took me to the very beginning and entertaining a thought about what if our whole life is a dream. Nature of dreams is a funny thing.

I was still in that room, on that floor. I was trying to... stay alive, I guess. I had to get out of there but where to go exactly? I hardly knew where I was.

I got up, started running a long hallway, then another one and another one. They were all empty looking the same with no one around. Every direction I took led to a dead end.

I didn't want to run anymore. So I just leaned on the wall and sat on the floor. I looked at both hallways. I started laughing. I laughed as hard as I could. I don't even know why. I laughed so hard that it started to hurt. So I laughed some more. Laughter is a beautiful thing. It makes our life longer and happier. Like love, like eating chocolate. You simply wish for it to last forever, if there is such a thing.

So I laughed and laughed away. I could say the whole world could hear me. I felt like a little kid who just wished to taste something sweet to be happy. A need for sweets shaped my state of mind. And now, there were all these tastes of sweet. It was as if I could've tasted it at that very moment, as I sat there on the floor.

Funny thing… you taste something like that and all of sudden a whole world becomes different. Or again, was it just, dare I say, all in my head?

Chapter 12

Next thing I knew, I opened my eyes. I was lying on a wooden floor. I felt pain. I had a terrible headache. It clouded my mind. It faded like a fog as I was getting to my senses.

I looked at the sunlight shining through the window. I touched my face with my hands. It was bloody. I looked at the stairs.

Right... Shit. What?

I remembered the fall... I didn't have anything broken. Was I on this floor this entire time? I guess I was. It can't be. Well, I guess it can. I tried to think, but I couldn't.

I tried to move, got up, and felt out of balance. I went to the bathroom and took a shower. I watched the blood going its way down the sink. I felt like I was aware of a body that wasn't mine. It was painful and weird. Like someone else's heart was beating.

Afterwards I wiped myself with the towel looking at it in a mirror. I looked at my body. I didn't actually go anywhere... Although I felt like I went to hell and back. I felt tight in my chest.

I put some clothes on and went out. It was a sunny day. People seemed to be doing their usual stuff. Yet again, I felt like I fell from Mars.

I walked till I came to the city. People were catching a day. They were walking, rushing, talking to each other. I looked at that sitting on some bench. Some people were with their pets, walking around, playing in the sun. That looked nice.

"Hey pal..." I heard someone. It was a friend of mine. "What's up?"

He was with his girlfriend. She looked nice.

"You all right?" he said.

"Yeah, I'm ok. How are you?"

"I'm ok."

I looked at him.

"So what's going on?"

"Not much. Just chilling in the sun."

"Ah, yes. It's a fine day. Well, give me a call. Let's do something together."

"Sure. Will do."

"All right man. See you."

"See you."

He took his girlfriend's hand while walking away. I looked at it.

"Hey…" I said.

He turned and looked at me.

"You two look good together."

My friend smiled and his girl too.

"Thanks."

I looked at him and smiled.

Sun shone over the city. Birds flew freely. There were no clouds, just pure, clear, pale-blue sky.

I kept looking around…and then I heard the church bell ringing. Church was at the square not far from where I was sitting. I stood up, started walking toward it. I went in, which I didn't intend to. It was quiet and empty. I stood there in silence for a few moments.

I started walking towards the altar. I went into a confession room.

I sat there in silence till I heard someone.

"Yes?"

"I… To tell you the truth I don't know why am I talking to you right now." A few moments passed in silence.

"I'm not a sinner," I said. "I can't remember the last time I've been here."

"Something led you here?"

"I had a dream."

"What was the dream about?"

"I went to this place… I went there for answers."

"What kind of answers?"

"I… was lost. I've lost my father."

"Did you find it there?"

"I thought I did. But you know, it was all right."

Moment passed in silence.

"Why do we lose it father? Why do we lose our faith?"

"What do you think faith is?"

"How about you tell me."

"You went to that place to discover it. What did you find?"

"I'm not sure if that's faith."

"It can be whatever you want to be. It is our choice to believe in whatever makes us going. Sometimes it gets odd and hard. That's when we have to find the strength and reasoning. Faith has its way of rewarding us."

"Do you believe in heaven and hell?"

"Do you?"

I went to church one time. I just sat there, looked around. And after a while I imagined an angel and devil having sex. I just smiled. I'm not a sinner but my thoughts surely are. I don't know…Maybe I'm just bored to death."

"Sounds like you are rediscovering your faith."

"Do you have justification for everything?"

"Just reasoning."

"What happens when it gets… challenged?"

"It's like a muscle. You work on it, you build it, make it stronger. Everything is a matter of practice, staying curious. It's like dancing."

I looked at the outline of his head on the other side.

"Who are you?"

"Just a voice of reason… Go with your instinct. Work on your curiosity. You will find your answers. Be persistent."

I went out, started walking towards the way out, looking back at it over my shoulder. I went out like I needed some fresh air or something. I looked at the sky. I looked at the sun. I felt warmth. I closed my eyes. There is a certain comfort in simplicity. As much as you could get lost, simplicity can guide and define your existence. I sensed that inside.

*

A few days later I called up my friend. He told me about a party.

I held a beer bottle, watching others drinking and talking. I had told my friend all about my dream.

"There's your novel man," he said. "And… you can actually go and find that place. Hell, I'll come with you."

I looked at him. "What about your girlfriend?"

He had some beer. "Don't worry about that. It'll be an adventure. Do you still have that map?"

"Yeah…"

I looked at others. Music was playing…

"What…" he said looking at me.

"Nothing… I just… All these people… Same lives, same jobs. Nothing changes. It's like drowning. It's fucking terrifying. It feels like a mouse running in a spinning circle. Faster he runs, more funny he looks, or foolish. Have you ever seen that? I see all these people's lives. It's like seeing puppets. I don't want to live like that. I just don't know where I fit in."

"Is that why you want to leave?"

"That's a part of it. I have to find out what is out there."

"What if you get hurt, like in the dream?"

"Man said it wouldn't happen the same way twice. You can't let yourself live in fear of everything that can be dangerous."

"What does that mean?"

"That means fuck it. Anything can happen to anybody at any given time."

He smiled. "That's what I like about you. You take things the way they are."

"How the fuck else can you take them? The thing is what you do about them."

"I'll tell you what we're gonna do about it… We are gonna have some fun," he laughed.

The booze came and some girls came. Not the kind of girl whom you would chat with. I wasn't particularly down for chatting. Talk was always the same and boring.

I felt like I was on the way of…becoming this…other person while looking at one of the girls going soft on me. I felt him more and more present like a force. Like energy.

The girl started unbuttoning my shirt. I was realizing I was free like in no other way I'd be. I was kind of far in my mind. I heard the sound, the sound in the distance. Don't know where I was. I was going over some land. I was reaching mountain tops. The land looked endless. Like the sky.

I felt her kisses on my chest as I was sitting, looking at her with the beer bottle in my hand. She was pretty. I wondered what her deal was... You can lose your sense of imitation. You have to be whoever you are. Otherwise it doesn't work.

There was this music in my head playing... as she was going all over me. I looked at her in her game. She was looking at me. At moments I saw us as two animals snuggling one to another, playing. She looked interesting, feminine. I tried to picture what animal she reminded me of? A she-wolf, black panther, lioness or some wild cat. It felt good as far as whatever that was I was feeling. I felt like I was going down in a deep, dark-blue sea. Seeing all that dark blue I remembered how I used to be scared of it when I was a kid. It kind of looked intimidating when you see it and think of it. But it's just a color. Like any other. Going deeper is much scarier. But you can't be scared. Fear can paralyze you and literally kill you. You can turn it into a force of resistance. It is up to you. So don't be afraid. Just face it and you'll realize how tough you really are.

Well, I was still in that deep, dark-blue... but not scared, just lost. I looked around and didn't see anything. Now, that's an odd feeling 'cause it feels like it takes forever. But nothing is forever. So they say.

I looked at the girl while being far in my thoughts. She started dancing slowly. I looked at her like a loosened spirit. I tried to imagine her in a story...

Chapter 13

I walked the road, hitchhiked. At some point, someone made a stop, some people in an old pickup truck. They were farmers or something of sort, wearing old shirts, jeans and hats, looking kind of westernish. They even gave me some food and beer. One of them played the guitar having his hat bended on his head along with another guy blowing into the accordion.

We drove all night among the clear sky and fresh air. We were the only ones on the road driving till early morning when we got to some town. A small town, looking empty. That was the place they were from.

They left me somewhere while dawn was coming. It was early and hot. I looked around where I could go. Streets were empty and everything was closed. So I took some direction and amazingly got to the beach.

Well, I saw a beautiful sunrise. I just dropped my things and lay on the sand. I looked at the waves, listened to sounds while the sun was making its way up. And then, I fell asleep.

When I woke up I felt a wind on my face. I took a look at a shore… I got up, walked to the water and washed my face with it. I had no idea where I was. But that feeling was sort of cool.

I took my things and went back to the town. I wandered the streets till I saw a place that looked like a bar or something. I went in. It was half empty. I sat in the booth. Then she came and greeted me with her look.

"What can I get you?"

"Coffee, please."

She went for it and came back with a big pitcher she started pouring from. Black liquid smoked in the air.

"You are not from around here…" she said.

"What makes you say that?"

"This is a small town. Everybody knows everybody. I haven't seen you around."

I had some coffee.

"What do you do?" she said.

I looked at her. "I'm a writer."

"Oh really? What do you write about?"

"Places I go… People I meet. Stuff that happens…" I smiled.

She looked at me smiling, looking pleasant.

"How long have you been here?"

"I just got here this morning."

"Oh, how do you like it so far?"

"It's… interesting I would say. What about you? Are you from here?"

"Yeah I live here with my brothers."

"Oh, that's interesting. Do they drive an old pickup truck?"

"They do. How do you know?"

"They picked me up on the road. I came with them."

"Oh, really? How long are you gonna stay?"

"Don't know. I guess I'll see what catches my fancy." I took a sip of coffee looking at her.

"Ok. Well… enjoy your coffee."

"Thanks. Can you tell me about a good place to stay?"

"Oh, sure. It's close to here."

It was a fair looking room in an apartment building with a view of mountains looking green through a fog of sunlight on a hot day. It looked picturesque. I'd dropped my things on the bed just looking at that through the window. I felt my soul light as that sunlight was, shining all round… I felt like I could watch that sight for the rest of my life without taking another breath. I took my notebook and wrote some words that came to mind. All the life around existed peacefully as it shaped me inside while the sun was setting down.

I got hungry. I walked back to that bar. There were more people there…

I sat at the counter. Girl came.

"You are still here?"

"Still here…" she said, evidently tired. "What can I get you?"

"Does the kitchen still work?"

"It does,"she said and handed me the menu.

I started looking over the dishes with a picture next to them.

"I'll go with the burger, thank you."

"Sure thing,"she said smiling.

I had a beer while I was waiting.

"So how do you like the place you're staying in?"

"It has an amazing view."

"I know…That's why I sent you there. You said you are a writer? What is it like to be one?"

"Well, I get to meet someone like you. I get to taste beer and burgers at this place of amazing scenery, heading towards what's gonna happen next. You always look for the story. Everything is a story and of course, how you tell it. What gives you the reason?"

"What's yours?"

"Well, I travel… and write. That's what I do. And now, I'm talking to you,"I said smiling. "Have you ever been in those woods?"

"Woods?"

"Up in the mountains."

"Yeah…"

"What is it like out there?"

"It's just the woods."

"Would you go with me?"

She looked at me.

"Why do you want to go there?"

"Just curious."

She kept looking…

"Ok…" she said. "My brothers will take us."

"Ok."

"Tomorrow."

"What are you doing after work?"

"Oh, I'm just gonna crash. I'm dead tired."

I smiled and had some beer. A bell rang. My burger was ready.

Later that night I couldn't sleep. Maybe because of the full moon. I was lying in the bed, in the dark, looking at it through the window. I felt odd about being at this place. I felt odd about that moon staring at me. I got up and walked out.

It was late and dark. I walked the street… looking around. I felt like I was the only one on the planet. Now, that was a funny feeling. I looked at my footsteps while listening to them. I looked at wooden houses in the dark. Wow… This place really looked like the end of the world or the end of something…

I kept walking and then somewhere along the way I heard something. Somebody else was walking. But I didn't see anyone. I took a better look and saw a puppy. It was a little puppy dragging something around his neck. It was a friendly one. He started to cry when he saw me.

He was a small, brown dog with a necklace around his neck with a leash on it.

"Hey little fellow… Where did you come from?"

He looked at me with his pretty, sad eyes. He licked my nose. I smiled and cuddled him.

"Who did you run from?"

He just looked at me with his tongue out wagging his tail.

"Come…Let's look where you got lost from."

I took him in my arms. He was quiet. He looked like he didn't know anything except being carried like he was in some adventure of his own. That made me smile. How about that? I had a friend. We just ran onto each other. That's how it happens sometimes. Funny thing, that is. I took a look at him and wondered was he hungry or thirsty? Of course he was. Dogs can always eat and drink. I wondered when was the last time he did that? Well, I didn't have food nor water so I just kept walking, hoping to run into someone.

The place looked like an old cowboy town. All dark and spooky surrounded with mountains looking like shadows and that full moon. In spite of looking all dark and spooky, it looked sort of romantic too. Maybe I just saw it that way.

I looked at the puppy. He looked sad but funny. I smiled and he smiled too.

"No one knows where we are, pal. Do you want to be found?"

He started barking. I noticed a house with a light on. Puppy growled.

"What's wrong pal? Is that it?"

He growled and barked. He snatched out of my arms and started rushing towards the door. He started jumping on them, scratching, crying. Door opened and a man walked out. He was old and skinny. He had short, gray hair. Dog jumped on him, crying. Man made a sound and the dog went quiet. He took a leash and looked at it. It was ripped off. Man looked at it and then looked at the puppy.

"Now, how in hell did this happen?"

Dog just looked at him, looking kind of scared.

"Sometimes I really wish you could talk," a man said.

Puppy laid his head on the floor like he was ashamed.

Man turned and looked at me.

"Where did you find him?"

"Down the street," I looked behind. "About an hour from here…"

"He's lucky. You are lucky," a man said, talking to the dog, pointing his finger at him. "Thank you, sir. I appreciate it," man said.

"Not a problem."

"You wanna come in for a beer or something?"

I looked at him for a second.

"Sure."

I went in along with a puppy. It was a small, simple looking house. Man opened a fridge, opened two beers and put them on the table.

"Cheers," he said.

Puppy jumped on a couch and lied there.

I had some beer looking around… trying to figure out who this man was and what he's doing here.

"So… What is this place?" I said after time passed in silence.

He had some beer going down his throat.

"This place?"

He took a pack of cigarettes, opened it and offered it to me.

"No, thank you."

He took one and lit it, pulling smoke in and out.

"Have you ever heard about those ghost towns?"

I nodded my head.

"This place used to be one. Then some people came. Some of them stayed, some left."

He took some more beer.

"What is it that you do?" he said. "If you don't mind me asking."

"I'm a writer."

"A writer... Interesting thing to know how to do. I've never met a writer before. You use words as your tools. It takes special skill for that. Well, what are you doing here? Far from everything..."

"I'm not quite sure. Sort of follow my curiosity. I kind of go where the story takes me."

He looked at me. "Give me your right hand."

I looked at him.

"It's all right. That's what I do," he said. "You saved my dog... Let me see."

I pulled it out. He took it and looked at it.

"You... will have a long life. You are a fighter. You're confused about your place in this world but that doesn't mean bad things for you. You will meet someone... someone special. But you'll have to figure out how to be with that someone."

"You see all that on a palm?"

"Oh, yes... That's my skill."

I looked at his hand, holding mine.

He looked at me.

"Do you believe in what I just told you?"

"I want to believe."

"Well... then that is what you make of it."

He looked at me. "Everything means something... It's all connected."

This sounded familiar. We looked at one another.

"Anyway... just me looking at your palm," he said.

I felt a strange presence inside. Like an animal instinct. Like a lion moving, looking around. I felt his strength. I felt his hunger. I felt the wilderness that makes him a hunter.

"You want another beer?" the man said.

"No... Thank you. I should go."

"Well, it was nice meeting you."

"You too."

"You take care now…"

I walked out. I was weakening… I was shaking. I was breathing heavily. I looked around but all I saw was dark. I felt like a blind man. I felt like going through dark woods. The one I dreamt about. As I was walking, I tripped and fell on the ground. I turned on my back. I looked at the sky. It was black. I felt better, coming to my senses. I was in the middle of nowhere… lying on the dusty ground, thinking about what man said, how everything is connected. I closed my eyes, feeling them heavy.

I felt a tongue licking me on my face… I heard a dog sniffing, waking me up. I saw that puppy again, climbing on my chest.

"Hey you… You lost again? What happened?"

I tried to get up, took a look around. But there was no dog. I scratched my head. Well, they don't call it a ghost town for no reason.

In time I got back, morning was coming. This place was strange and forsaken but it surely had its beauty while the sun was rising, glowing over the odd land of mountains, woods and ground of dust.

I took a shower, took my notebook and wrote some more. I looked at the sight. All that land. It was so peaceful and quiet. No sound at all, almost a bit scary or simply legendary.

I went to the bar for lunch. I sat at the counter. Girl saw me and came. I nodded my head.

"How's it going," I said.

"All right… How are you?"

"Ok, thanks."

"You look… different," she said.

"Yeah… I had an odd night."

"Oh, what happened?"

"Nothing… I just… I've met an old man up on a hill."

"An old man… oh, a fortune teller."

"I ran into his puppy on the street with a leash ripped off."

"Yes, he's very attached to his dog. You want me to bring you anything?"

"Yeah… same as last time, thank you."

She brought me beer.

"So you still want to go up in the woods?" she said.

"Yeah."

"I've talked to my brothers. We can go tomorrow."

"Ok. What are you doing later?"

She looked at me. "Why?"

"Just thinking… we could go to the beach or something if you want."

"Ok,"she said after a few moments.

Later that day we went to the beach. She looked completely different and dressed casually. Like a different person. She was hot and natural. I just looked at her bathing in the sun with her eyes closed. With her loosened darkish-blonde hair. Her body was all sweaty and shiny while the sun was setting, leaving the sky in color of pink behind.

I wanted to save that moment but I couldn't take the photo or anything like that. I didn't have a phone nor anything else. All I had was that notebook and the pen.

So, I started drawing, although I wasn't much of a drawer, but that was all I had.

I was drawing her sort of feeling like making love to her.

Later she fell asleep. And I went into the water, leaving my notebook on a towel.

I dived, floated on my back, and looked at the sky. Then she woke up and went in.

"I drifted off…sorry,"she said.

"No worries. I loved watching you sleeping,"I smiled.

She smiled back.

"So what is it about you and this town?"

"What do you mean?"

"Well, you're… young, smart, obviously good looking."

"I don't know…I thought about it but never actually did it."

I looked at her.

"I'm pretty close with my brothers. They have been taking care of me since the very day I can remember. This place… My folks had met somehow. They came here. This was a town of ghosts with literally no one. That suited some people Anyway… I didn't know them. All I know is what my brothers have told me. Folks had land which my brothers inherited. I have no school. No education. All I know, I've learned from brothers."

"You are lucky to have them."

She smiled. "Yeah."

"Well... Maybe I could take you."

"Where?"

"Wherever you want to go."

"I can't just leave them. Not like that."

"I understand."

"How long are you going to stay?"

"Don't know."

It got dark with no lights around, just a clear sky.

"What are you thinking about?" she said.

"Nothing..."

"Are you hungry? I can make us some food."

"Sure. That's very kind of you."

We went to her place. And she made some food. It was beautiful watching her. She played us some Spanish music, poured us some wine.

"Your brothers play too," I said.

"They do..."

"They sound pretty good."

"You've heard them playing?"

"I have... on our way here."

"Hm... You should hear me singing."

"I definitely would."

She licked her fingers and set the food on the table, poured some more wine and lit the candles. She wore a dress, looking sensational in it.

"Wow...you are pretty good at this," I said.

"I don't get to do it often."

"You didn't have to go through all that trouble."

"It's not trouble when you like it."

"Touche."

We sat at the table, had some food and some wine while music was playing. She looked at me and I looked at her.

"What?" I said.

"Nothing..." she smiled. "Just thinking about quitting the job. Do something with my brothers. It makes sense to me right now."

"You should. You should give it a shot at least. You never know what door would open for you."

"Now you speak like a fortune teller," she smiled.

"You talked to him?"

"He came by to the bar, a couple of words here and there. He doesn't talk much, but when he does it always means something."

"You believe in that stuff?"

"I don't know... Sometimes it makes perfect sense, other times it sounds like someone else's life."

She had some wine.

"You know how that is. I mean being a writer. Putting yourself in someone else's shoes. Imagining being somebody else."

I took a piece of food in my mouth.

"Yeah... It's different every time. It's like an inner thing. You sort of get access to it and sometimes it's like a locked room you can't get out of."

"What do you do then?"

"Well... you try to be creative. Try to put yourself in that state of mind, see what it tells you. Eventually, if it's supposed to happen, it'll happen."

"How far did you go?"

"I don't know... What is far?"

She smiled and had some wine. I stood up and got close to her. I pulled out my hand.

"Would you like to dance?"

She gave me her hand and got up. We started dancing. After a while of dancing with her I felt like I could do it forever. In my mind I have.

"I could go like this forever," she said.

She surely had some moves. She felt free with me as I was with her. We danced the whole night, smiling, drinking... looking at one another. I lifted her up, she chuckled holding my arms. She pulled her head back. She closed her eyes and stretched her hands wide like she was flying. She looked incredible while music played wildly.

I put her on the ground.

"Where did u go?"

"Everywhere..." she looked at me smiling. She was getting close to me slowly and kissed me. I kissed her back. And then she just looked at me all serious while music kept playing. She laid her hands on my cheeks.

"Why so serious?" I said.

"I'm just thinking, am I going over my head with this?"

"Don't think of it that way. You are a beautiful, good looking woman. It's easy with me and I'm not a serial killer or anything like that," I smiled.

"Wow… Well, that's comforting. Maybe I am."

"Interesting. You must be the hottest serial killer I've ever seen. I may find a story there."

"I would say you already have."

She kissed me again, long and sweet.

"Good enough?"

"Oh, I have a very short memory… Can you do it again?"

She smiled and did it again. I melted inside. I felt strangely present. I felt light as the air I was breathing.

And so we kissed while music was playing. Till late. The sky was getting brighter outside and all that land was being seen as magical again. Well, let me tell you… It takes oddly little to be happy. They say it's a state of mind. They could be right. It's not about what you wish for. It's what you have. It's a state of appreciation. Different things make different people happy. The thing is, it all comes and goes. So what is it about being happy? You can be happy one moment and sad the next. It's how you perceive the moment of now. That is really all you got.

We looked at the sight through the window, having glasses of wine in our hands.

I looked at her. "Thank you for a wonderful dinner."

She smiled. "You're quite welcome."

We kept looking while music was still playing.

Then we went for a shower. Long one, if you know what I mean.

Later on we went outside. Day was sunny as we were walking the street. An old pickup truck was parked nearby. One of the brothers was sitting at the back, playing his guitar. He was playing it slowly, subtly. He was dressed like a cowboy. I couldn't see his face clearly. He had sunglasses and a hat on.

"What are you playing?"

"Stuff that comes," he said.

"Interesting. Where did you learn how to play?"

"I don't talk much about it. I just play." He played some more while I watched it.

"You want to go to the woods," he said. "You know what you want to do there?"

"Stuff that comes," I said mildly smiling.

He smiled too. "We'll take you there but we can't stay. We got to go."

"Ok."

"Jump in."

We went for a ride. I looked at all the land around. It looked like a no man's land.

They left us somewhere on the way, told us they'll pick us up on their way back.

I wasn't really sure what I was doing. I just followed the feeling of simply being out there. She followed me in silence, stepping lightly.

"Tell me something about these parts."

"There is not much really to tell," she said. "It is what it is. Sun rises, sun sets."

I smiled. "Interesting choice of words."

Now she smiled.

"Have you ever been lost?" I said.

"Lost?"

"Like did you always know your place in the world?"

"Place in the world… I don't really know how to think about the world. So I don't."

"I had a dream about being lost in a place like this. And now I feel strangely present in the present."

"Is that why you wanted to come here?"

"I was just curious. It looked so amazing from my window."

"It is amazing I guess. Kind of like there's a secret to it," she said.

"There surely is."

At some point of walking we found ourselves at the plain sight of dry land spreading wide, with nothing around but red rocks and mountains looking grand on sun that was slowly going its way down.

We looked at that. We looked around while I sat on the ground.

"Are you all right?" she said.

"Yeah, I just have a feeling I'm on some other planet."

"I know what you mean."

She started to sing while we looked at it. She sounded beautiful as if all that land could hear her. Well, maybe it could as much as we knew. I knew one thing. This sight was waking life inside. So I sat there watching the sight and her singing as if I was going to live forever.

Sun was going down shining its light on the ground while she was still singing up until the moment we saw the last of it sinking. And then, it was simply silent. Wind started to blow.

I looked at that and got up. I came to her and looked at her.

"You have an amazing voice."

"Thank you," she said, smiling.

I kissed her while the wind was getting stronger. Then there was thunder, and another one...

"We better go back," she said.

I looked at the sky, I looked at her. I took her hand and strangely felt like I was back at that party again. I was dancing with the girl while some slow song was on.

I started laughing.

"What's funny?" she said.

"Nothing... I'm laughing at myself."

"Why?"

"No reason. I just went to some ghost town and back. I've met you there."

"Me? What's a ghost town?"

"Very special place I could take you there someday."

"Cool," she said. "What about right now?"

"What?"

"Now... What do you wanna do now?"

"Let me show you." I reached out and kissed her. She kissed me back. I honestly felt like I could fly away. I felt like my mind was hotwired. I felt this was the very reason to be alive.

"I have an idea," she said.

She went up to my friend and started talking to him. Next thing I know, we were in a car, driving the city. Someone took some booze from the party and now bootless were going from hand to hand. I was sitting at the back seat just looking out... having a feeling I was looking at it through the camera or something. Another thought that entertained me, when nothing else could.

Now, I didn't take anything, but that was a trip my mind projected on its own. So now, I was looking at everything like some kind of a movie. That was kind of cool. My friend had put the music on. I looked at them all like actors.

We drove to some street, parked near the place. It was a place with loud music coming from inside. We got out of the car, crossed the street and walked in. Place was packed with people dancing, jumping with their hands in the air.

A band was playing live. A few of them were jamming on stage. They sounded raw and exciting. Yet I felt the world is coming to an end.

I got to the bar and ordered a beer. I looked at all the people feeling like I was in some kind of video game. I felt my body and mind like someone else's. I looked at my hands like someone else's. Then I felt strangely excited, strangely driven.

Then a girl came.

"Come, let's dance," she said smiling, taking my hand.

She took me dancing. And boy did I dance. I danced like there was no tomorrow. I made her laugh and everybody around. I even went singing with the band. We rocked the place so much that I felt it was going to crash. I yelled into the microphone, singing. Crowd was jumping. I felt like a rock star. I jumped in a crowd. They carried me. I felt this thing inside let's call it life, going wild. It's... strange when you feel like being someone else. I had a feeling I was going to fade. My mind and body were on fire.

I drank some more, danced some more. She appeared from somewhere among the crowd. We danced snuggled to one another. Our hands were loosened. Mine were all over her. She bent her head on my shoulder from behind. Dancing can extend your life and you kinda wish for the party to last forever. Well, maybe that's just me.

I had to go to the bathroom so I left. I came to one of the urinals and it started leaking. I was drunk, I was horny. My stomach was turning. I heard the devil inside me laughing. I felt my head heavy like a motherfucker.

I came to the sink, started washing my hands and face. I watched the drops falling off it in the mirror.

Then she came… walking in slowly, looking at me. I looked at her in the mirror.

"This is a man's toilet," I said, smiling.

"I know. Do I look like I care?" she said like she couldn't care less and locked it.

I turned, crossed my hands and looked at her.

She came closer. "So who was I?"

"What?"

"That ghost town where you said you'd met me?" she said nonchalantly.

"A girl in a story."

"Sounds exciting." She looked at me.

"It is."

"How does it end?"

"It doesn't."

"A story without an end? What kind of story is that?"

"Ongoing one"

She smiled. "It's funny… I'm looking at you but it's like I can see all kinds of different people."

"Yeah I'm funny that way." I smiled.

"Tell me more."

"My mind is on fire but blank at the same time. I would rather show you."

She looked at me like she was trying to figure me out. She had her lips closer to mine. I sensed her smell. I looked at her eyes.

Someone banged on the door.

"You wanna get out of here?" she said.

She took my hand and we went out. We started going through the crowd. But then I lost her. It was like her hand slipped from mine. All of sudden I felt lost among that crowd of people. I looked for her but I didn't see her. I looked at all the faces around. I started feeling something like smothering inside. I started breathing heavily. I hated crowds.

I fought my way through and I went out on the street. I looked around. The street was empty. I saw a few people nearby. They were drinking and smoking. I asked them if they'd seen the girl… I didn't know her name, so I described her. They said they didn't. I looked inside through the window waiting for her to appear. The fresh air suited me. I looked at the black sky and started thinking about something else.

I didn't feel like going inside. I felt like walking... so I started to walk. I walked the streets aimlessly. They were dark, cold and empty. I just walked, feeling kind of odd and silly.

I walked till the break of dawn, the quietest time on the planet.

I came home, the quietest place on the planet. I climbed the stairs, came into my room. Morning sun shone over the land. I came to the window and looked at it. I've heard someone say there's a certain therapeutic effect to this. A chemical reaction in the brain that affects the entire body to heal and be happy. Now, that's simply amazing. It works, it's free, and you don't have to do much, just watch. Well, except for waking early, if you want to split hairs.

I looked at that sight, feeling how my mind reacted. I felt a kind of comfort that everything will be alright somehow. I guess time will tell.

I turned and saw a sketch and the map on the table. I came to it and sat on the chair. I took it in my hand and looked at it. Then I looked at the clock on the wall. I heard it's ticking... It was the only sound in the room. That got me thinking. I looked at it with this odd feeling that time is running out. It runs to the inevitable. Well, that doesn't necessarily mean a bad thing if you don't think about it. It's like the Man said "It's all about finding the way", whatever the way that is.

I looked at the clock ticking, holding the sketch and the map in my hands, sitting in silence with the ticking, the only sound I heard. This sound can make you go insane.

I took a deep breath. Well, I have to figure out what the rest of my life is going to look like. But let's say I have an idea. And that is a start. You can always start from somewhere.

www.ingramcontent.com/pod-product-compliance
Lightning Source LLC
Chambersburg PA
CBHW031553310726
48973CB00003B/803